THE GOLD SARCOPHAGUS

Paul M. Vander Loos

ACKNOWLEDGEMENTS

I would like to acknowledge the excellent cover art shown on this edition as well as the other two books of the series by Irish artist Michael Lenehan whose work can be found on the DeviantArt site http://mick2006.deviantart.com and his email is micklenehan2002@yahoo.co.uk. Thanks also go to my friends and readers who have waited patiently for the third book in the *Nine Worlds* series to finally reach publication status.

A VISION OF RA

Between the tiniest particles spanning the universe are sinuous passages that appear and disappear in random flashes, momentarily linking vast distances of space that can then be traversed in minutes. However, no intelligent being has been able to stabilise these minute portals for long enough and in such a way as to allow the passage of beings and objects much too large for such microscopic dimensions. Nerthulians have long dreamed of such things but are at a loss to realise it. Such imaginings are relegated to the realms of wild fantasies. The Nerthulians also debate the existence of any other intelligence in the universe, unaware they are related to an alien master race who call themselves the Universal Guardians or Uranians. In their ancestry are a mysterious group of immortals who are simply referred to as the Ancients, whose knowledge is the source of the creation of the Werdstone and the Three Stones of Destiny, and the portal links that allow full-size beings to traverse between them and other lesser crystal structures. The portals remain open for moments at a time and possess dangerous side effects that will rob anyone using them without suitable protection of their memories. The Three Stones of Destiny that link these portals comprise Oashu, which the Ancients placed on Mirrortac's home planet of Mareos; Darm, which connected Mareos with the unstable and hostile planet of Thenigmas; and Einuk, which sank down with Atlantis on the planet of Nerthule. Under instruction from his guardian spirit, Phantac, Mirrortac and his family have taken Oashu and Darm which now are locked together at the former palace of the rebel demi-god Yidu. The last stone remains in Nerthule where scientists have located it in a golden sarcophagus recovered from the bottom of the sea. The power of these stones is immense, and in unwise hands, will corrupt the user.

* * *

Mirrortac's white fur stirred in the soft breeze of the mesa. His green eyes took in the distant landscape that before had been manipulated under a complex matrix of spells to form the bizarre and hostile micro-world of Skye. Cat-like ears twitched as he heard the voices of the large, equally furry hyfnuks of his ancestor race, the roznoghs. They were climbing up a long twine ladder they had constructed themselves to enable passage to the lowland below the mesa cliffs. Each was burdened with bitter vegetables, fruits and creatures they had gathered and hunted amid the now quiet groves of trees and gentle valleys stretching out to the far reaches of Skye. Without the sorcery of their former 'god' Yidu, Skye was less a place to fear and more one to enjoy. Its climate was certainly more temperate than the icy wastelands that the roznoghs called home. The hyfnuks were taller and stronger than many of their brothers and sisters, and therefore given the task of hunting and gathering for their people's food.

A cool nose nuzzled up against his neck as his she-one, Ameece, a roznogh herself, and once the guardian of the Werdstone, approached from behind. Her fur too was white, but natural, unlike Mirrortac's whose fur was originally a dark grey, but over time had been transformed through a rainbow of colours until this recent transformation.

'Where be your heart now, warrior of mine?' she whispered, her breath warm with the aroma of fruit.

'You know my heart be always with you, rainbow of my heart,' he smiled.

'I know that,' she said. 'But I feel you yearn for another place, another time.'

The erfin winced at the rheumatism in his leg. 'I have travelled far from my homeland, Eol, and my kinsfolk. But I fear it be naught my time to return. If I shall ever return.'

Ameece pulled his face towards her and looked into eyes that betrayed his age in the wrinkles that cob-webbed out from their corners.

'We were both very different in those days in Eol, when I was Yenic in my former life.'

Mirrortac looked away. 'There be yet a stone in Nerthule. The mission is incomplete.'

'But Yidu has been taken to stand before his people. He has no power to possess the Nerthulians anymore.'

The erfin shook his head. 'I know of this. What more is there now that he be gone? Yet ... it nags me.'

A series of grunts interrupted their talk, as first one, then other coarse black heads emerged from the edge of the cliff line. The hyfnuks shouldered their loads easily yet were somewhat out of breath after the long climb.

Daghva was the first of the hyfnuks to approach and bowed slightly before them while he adjusted his load.

'We have brought much to eat ... and some old friends of yours,' he said with a wink.

The elder erfin gave him a bemused look.

'You shall see. They are coming shortly,' Daghva said.

Daghva bowed again before continuing towards the crystal palace, with four other hyfnuks following close behind him. Mirrortac peered expectantly at the edge of the mesa where the hyfnuks had emerged to see who these 'old friends' would be and was soon rewarded as three winged creatures flung themselves over the top and ambled up towards them. The familiar gibbon faces were that of the tree-dwelling faugs whose community lived next to Skye for many generations. The one in the lead was carrying a stoppered vial marked with an inscription on its wooden surface.

'Forgive us oh wondrous sorcerer. We accused you of dark intentions, but we knew nothing of your great mission to rid us of the evil Yidu. Your deeds will be told in our tales for our descendants to pass on.' The faug's eyes were downcast as he awaited the erfin's reply.

Mirrortac patted the faug's shoulder.

'There be naught to forgive, my faug fellow.'

The faug lifted the vial and proffered it to the elder erfin. 'We know of the essence of Yu that has untangled the tongues of you and your child-fins, but the roznogh here has none. I suggest you all take a sip of this our own essence of Yu which is of an older recipe than that of our faug kin in the great forest. It has something more to offer you that the forest essence will not. It will join all your minds and reveal the minds of others. There are few who can drink of this essence ... only the greatest among us.'

Ameece returned the bow. 'You honour us! Blessings upon you winged ones.'

Mirrortac accepted the vial, bowing deeply in return.

'I be greatly honoured.'

'Come and feast with us! Our hyfnuk folk have brought us much to eat,'Ameece invited.

They all made their way to the palace, which sparkled in the sunlight as its many shards and cylinders struck out at the sky. Parts of it were broken, and it was through a schism in one of the walls that they could enter the main hall where rows of columns stood, some leaning while a few had been sheared in two from the battle with Yidu's dragon.

It was still an impressive edifice despite the jumble of broken columns and the shards of crystal that had been roughly swept to one corner of the hall. The faugs gaped at the massive palace and its fluted roofline and turned to each other to chatter in their native tongue about what they saw around them.

'Even from such evil does some beauty come,' the head faug said.

Ameece nodded. 'I would like to think that there was some good in Yidu, though he be corrupted,' she said.

'It is true that the Werdstone could make one feel as though no-one could resist you. I have felt its numbing power myself,' Mirrortac admitted. 'And yet it was not that way with you, precious one.'

'That is curious,' she said with knitted brow.

They had reached the table where all the gathered food was placed, and the faugs were encouraged to be seated and eat. The feasting began with much excited chatter and grins as the faugs revealed jugs of mead that all eagerly accepted. The feasting went on for some time until the faugs decided it was time to return to their home forest. The head faug led them up one of the ragged crystal chutes that had been used as an exit for Yidu's sacred chuffs – the tall bird-beings who formerly guarded the palace. The surface inside the chute had been roughened to allow the chuffs to easily scale it to the roofline where they could then take off on their scouting missions over Skye.

The faugs easily made it to the roofline where they could launch themselves into a long glide across the fields of Skye and quickly return to their forest on the other side of Skye and at the edge of the homeland of the roznoghs – Yidrogh.

* * *

Mirrortac, Ameece and the others retired to their chambers where they slept until the late afternoon sunlight cast shadows across the floor. Mirrortac and Ameece then made their way to the main hall where they relaxed beside the gem-encrusted throne where one of their triplets, Ezof, already sat munching on some fruit. They were all enjoying the silence of the dusk when Ameece noticed something strange happening. She stared at the tiny slivers of crystal that tinkled and jumped up from the floor as a mysterious breeze entered the palace. The ceiling and the walls started to shudder, and a rumble rose from within the air near the Werdstone pedestal. Ameece rose to her feet, grabbed Mirrortac by the arm and glanced around quivering. Ezof stopped chewing and discarded the fruit seed. The other two triplets, Treetam and Mitac, ran in from the nearby hallway, armed with their solar-bite weapons. The rumbling grew into a roar and the air churned and darkened. They exchanged questioning stares as a translucent form coalesced in front of the Werdstone. Mirrortac frowned as he and the others recognised an alien figure forming within the magical storm. Colours flexed in and out as the figure floated for moments and seemed to regard them with emotionless eyes. They could not see him distinctly, but enough to discern that he was wearing a golden robe and a crown of gold in a circular disc, and he had three eyes like

Yidu, only the third one was golden.

They all watched him as the image of the man shunted across from the Werdstone and out towards a column at the back to the main hall. The ghostly figure did not maintain a proper form, moving instead in a flickering curtain of light like sunshine shunted through leaves that were moving in the breeze. The spectre moved on and disappeared through the column, taking the storm and the noise with it.

Ameece stared back at the spot where the vision had disappeared. 'Another of these gods, or whatever manner of being?' she said, screwing up her face.

'I would guess this other three-eye be from Nerthule. It seems I have yet to finish what has begun,' Mirrortac said.

'*We* must finish it, dada ... I grow bored here,' Ezof quickly added, and his brother and sister nodded their agreement.

'I shall also go wherever you are my dear erfin.' Ameece nudged him fondly. 'You will not lose me so easy in this my new life. I too know some tricks that as Yenic I had naught.'

Mirrortac smiled at her. 'Yeah, we knew not of such worlds as these when in Eol.'

'But what of Nerthule? Be it not across the Greater Sky? We will need Wa-ku and his flying ship to cross there,' Mitac pointed out.

Mirrortac indicated the Werdstone perched on its pedestal. 'We have use of the gateway.'

Treetam, the only female of the triplets, smirked. 'We shall all lose our minds, dada!'

Mitac nodded. 'Treetam is right, dada. Just use it to contact Wa-ku and he will come and take us there.'

Mirrortac trudged up the few steps to the pedestal to regard the Werdstone. 'How do you use this to talk to Wa-ku?' He fiddled vainly with the mechanisms surrounding it.

'Here, I will show you.' Ameece came up to him and operated one of the dials on the rim. 'You move this here to talk to Wa-ku. This one was for Darm ... Yidu used this to send you to Thenigmas. And this other is Nerthule – the Einuk stone. There be others here, but I know naught of them.'

Mirrortac waited for a reaction from the stone after Ameece had dialled in the address to Wa-ku, but nothing happened.

'It be useless,' he grumbled.

Ameece rolled her eyes. 'Oh you, so clever sorcerer! Place your hand on the stone. Your mind is still in Thenigmas with the wild ones!'

Mirrortac placed a furry hand on the stone which immediately filled up with a cloudy light before forming into the image of Wa-ku. A blond-haired head smiled back at him through sparkling azure eyes.

'You miss me already my erfin friends. I am still on my way to the Halls of Ra with my brother.'

Mirrortac came straight to the point. 'Be there others of the three-eye?'

Wa-ku hesitated as he stared back. '… err … what makes you ask such a thing? Yes, there are many tresoculi as we know them. Our race is composed of the duoculi such as I, and the tresoculi, who are born with extra abilities. Together we are the Uranians.'

'We have seen another three-eye pass through the palace here … he is like a spectre, with a crown of gold like the sun. We all saw him pass through and disappear.'

Wa-ku frowned, shaking his head. 'What? That cannot be! Are you certain you saw this being? Was he wearing a golden robe?'

Mirrortac nodded. '… with a golden third eye.'

Yidu's voice could be overheard in the background. 'He has awoken! Ra has awoken! We will rise up again!'

Wa-ku snarled back at his brother who was off-screen. 'Shut up!' he said before turning back towards the screen, his face ashen. 'This is indeed disturbing news. You saw Ra, who was the most powerful tresoculi of all the history of our planet Kosmo. The Council of Atlantis exiled him to Nerthule many thousands of years ago, and he was assumed killed in the great drowning of the city that the Nerthulians also called Atlantis. Somehow, he has preserved himself through his abilities, and has re-animated. This is a matter that I must bring to the attention of the Council as it may threaten the order of the cosmos.'

'Then we must be about finishing this mission. There is the third stone, Einuk, yet to gather on Nerthule. You must take us there!'

Wa-ku shrugged in apology. 'I am on my way to Kosmo. By the time I have told of Yidu's deeds and the council meets to consider what to do with him, and the matter of Ra, much time will have passed. Besides, though you impress me as a mere erfin in defeating my brother, Ra is a vastly different matter. He is many times more powerful than Yidu. You cannot risk it.'

'I must risk it. The mission is not complete.' Mirrortac's face was set.

Wa-ku sighed. 'Then you must wait. I will be gone many many days as you count them.'

The elder erfin balled his hand into a fist and slammed it down on the side of the pedestal, startling the others.

'There be naught time to wait. We must take the gateway.'

'How can you take the portal, Mirrortac? You cannot lose your mind again!'

'There must be a way. How be it that this Ra travels through it and yet keeps his mind?'

Wa-ku stroked his chin in thought. 'I know little about how the portals work, but I do know someone who is well studied in such things. I will get her to contact you.'

'Good! Get that someone to tell me; now to end this talk.' Mirrortac frowned at the apparatus before turning imploring eyes to Ameece.

She could just smile as she took his hand and placed it back on the stone. 'Why be you so foolish, my erfin. Here ... just put your hand here and brush the stone.'

Wa-ku's image chuckled as Mirrortac fidgeted with the stone before it all grew cloudy again, diminishing back to the dark lustre of the inactive crystal.

Mirrortac stood deep in thought as he struggled with some memory. 'Ra ... I know of this name. The Meretees people I met on the island of Plumer-Ra gave homage to him.' The elder erfin shivered. 'I remember the Astellites ... strange ones. They could display the suns and worlds in the Greater Sky on a stone dish many erfin-lengths in size. And Atlantis! I had visions of many Nerthulians dying as the Monsters of the Deep Earth shook their palaces and sent it into the endless lake. This is all the doing of Ra. Great Mateote! Wa-ku is right!'

The erfin related how the Meretees people had built a great pyramid at one end of the main island, and it was there that he met with the friendly and wise Ra-finelles who were keepers of the pyramid and its peculiar connection to Nerthule, which was broken when Atlantis fell. One of the Ra-finelles, Twx, took him up the mountain to meet the Astellites – an all female sect who kept a record of the Greater Sky, with all its many suns and planets. Crystal arrays powered the images that were displayed on the Pool Stones – the huge stone dishes that magnified the cosmos on their smooth surfaces. Twx and Mirrortac were forced to make a hasty departure after some evil power took hold of the Astellites and the gloomy statues that haunted the entrance. And it was soon after that the erfin had lost track of Twx and came upon a beach that finally led him to another journey to the sorcerers' world of Hopocus.

The erfin had just finished speaking when a voice issued from the Werdstone. They all hurried up to see another image of a Uranian woman whose auburn hair fell in voluminous silk locks past her shoulders. She had a freckled pale skin and blue eyes with streaks of green through the irises.

'My, my, so you are the erfins! So much hair; just how do you take care of it all?' She grinned widely, showing perfect teeth.

The triplets chuckled at the young woman and her peculiar manner. Ameece also smiled. But Mirrortac took no notice.

'Do naught concern yourself with fur. Do you know of the gateway and how we can travel to Nerthule without losing our minds?' he asked.

'Oh ... yes. Sorry. My name is Fayth, and you are this Millertuk, I assume,' she said, composing herself.

'Mirrortac ... I am Mirrortac,' he corrected. Now, of the gateway ...?' he urged.

'Sorry ... Mirrortac. I mustn't have heard Wa-ku right. Never mind. Yes, the portal ... I should be able to help you. You must find some headgear ... you know ... like crowns. They are special ones made for the purpose of portal travel ... because, as you say, you would all lose your minds. The helmet must be of alumi-metal mixed with gold. Yidu must have some there in his palace.'

Mirrortac scratched his head. 'Hmmm. I have naught seen such crowns.' He turned to the others. 'Do you know of what she speaks?'

'I have seen some shiny things in one of the chambers. Perhaps they are the helmets,' Treetam piped up.

'Yes ... sounds like them!' Fayth said. 'But you cannot take any weapons or other metal. The portal will spit you out into the void, and you'll die.'

'No solar-bites?' Ezof pouted.

'Especially no solar-bites. They will interfere with the stream.' Fayth gestured 'no' with her index finger and shook her head vigorously.

'Then how do we fight off any enemies?' Ezof asked.

'And how will we contact Wa-ku?' Mitac chimed in.

'We will not fight. All we need is the stone,' Mirrortac insisted.

Fayth frowned. 'Easy said. I fear you will die in Nerthule.'

Mirrortac just gave a confident smirk. 'There be great danger. But we will not die.'

'You are brave, I must say. Wa-ku sure was right about you, Mirrortac,' Fayth said.

Ameece bit her lip as she looked at her erfin but said nothing.

'Then, be there anything other for us to know of this gateway?' Mirrortac pressed.

'Yes, someone must operate the Werdstone ... someone who is not going to Nerthule. The others of you who are going must stand close together and hold hands ... tightly. And don't let go until you are in Nerthule. The stream is narrow and will appear as you go and disappear behind you. If one of you is not in the stream, then you will die in the void instantly.'

There was a stunned nodding of heads as they took in what Fayth said.

'Otherwise, your journey will be quick and safe. That's about it. Oh, and there should be a pendant under the Werdstone pedestal. One of you can wear it to communicate with Wa-ku,' she said. 'Mmmm, what I wouldn't give for some of that lovely fur of yours!' Fayth added.

Mirrortac looked askance at the others. 'And what would you do with such fur? It would keep you warm. You are all such hairless ones.'

Fayth laughed. 'Oh yes ... hee hee. But no, it would make such great wigs. We would wear them on our heads.'

Mirrortac chuckled. 'I have seen and heard much weirdness. And now hairless ones who wear fur on their heads where there be already fur!'

'Oh, it's a fashion thing. When we want to have a different style or colour.' Fayth's eyes lit up and she grinned widely.

The elder erfin bowed at the young woman. 'You are much help. Perhaps we can send you some of our fur for your head,' he said, grinning.

Fayth laughed in her light bubbly way, endearing her to them all.

'That'll be fantastic! You can give some to Wa-ku when you see him next.'

* * *

The caldera drifted into night, lit only by the feeble light of thousands of stars that burned like campfires of the gods in the velvet veil of the cosmos. Robed figures wearing star-shaped helms made silent passage between tall pillars from which stood the statue forms of Uranians. The 12 gathered around the concave smooth surface of an oval Pool Stone as crystal arrays in each of several domed chambers glowed a violet hue until their light concentrated on similar arrays around the oval concave, creating a magnified projection of the night sky on the smooth reflective stone surface. The Astellites had watched this process for the thousands of nights over the seasons of their lives and were accustomed to the images of suns and planets that floated across the stone screen.

But this night was different.

The images abruptly grew murky and dark, finally disappearing altogether as though a cloud had obscured the sky. Whiskers twitched on a seal-like face as the Sister of the Seventh Celestial Night ordered one of her Astellite kin to adjust a lever alongside the Pool Stone. The other Astellite obeyed, trying to manipulate the lever to clear the image but to no effect. Eau peered up at the sky to see a clear view of stars. She wandered between crystal arrays, hastily checking each for flaws, but found none. A dark mist was developing within the confines of the stone, gradually rotating with a hum that echoed throughout the courtyard and the cross-pattern of domes, pillars and marblelite gateways. Soft gasps rose among the Astellites who were backing away from the stone. Eau felt the freshness of the wind against her face and tugging at her dark robe. The hum intensified, building into a grinding noise as the wind quickened, brushing up leaves and rustling the vines that twisted around the gateways and pillars. The Astellites huddled together as the roaring tumult pushed at them. The dark vortex of mist formed a funnel that twisted and hovered over the Pool Stone. Crackles of light zig-zagged within the cloud until the Astellites were forced to shield their faces from a dazzling light that took shape from the centre of the vortex. Out of it stepped a man whose proud features spoke of royalty. A bright gold disc shone from a crown upon his head while his three eyes scrutinised the 12 who all fell to the ground and prostrate themselves before their Ra.

The tumult rapidly dissipated, leaving only the Uranian visitor and the Astellites trembling under their robes.

Ra regarded the Astellites from under painted eyes. A shining gold robe glistened as he strode over to Eau who kept her forehead close to the tiled courtyard.

'You please me my sisters. You may rise.'

Eau was first to slowly lift herself up, keeping eyes downcast as she and the others stood before their god. Without looking up, Eau said, 'Oh great and mighty Ra. How long we have awaited your return.'

'Humble sisters, Ra shines upon you with greetings of great import. You were chosen to complete my magnificent plan that will reunite all your kin across the cosmos. Have you and your sisterhood gathered the necklet stones as ordained upon your ancestors?'

Whispers of excitement flew up among them. 'We are greatly honoured to be the ones to deliver the necklet stones. They are, as pre-ordained, stored in the Elim chamber,' Eau said, stealing a peek at her god while still bowing her head.

'Then, take me there,' Ra said, his rich deep voice flowing from between lips both cunning and arrogant.

Eau led him to one of several interconnected domed chambers in which there was a large crystal cluster set upon a small platform and in plain sight of the concave of the Pool Stone. She pushed on one side of the array, which gradually slid across the marblelite floor, revealing an opening with a ladder that descended into a dark space. Ra followed down the ladder into a large room that twinkled with thousands of reflections. Eau lit a torch on a nearby wall, and they were immediately dazzled by the reflections from innumerable amethyst shadow crystals that took up almost all the space in the room from floor to ceiling.

Ra looked upon the small crystals with pleasure, smiling down at the Astellite sister. 'Ra looks upon you with favour. You and your sisters have done well.'

He picked up one of the crystals and examined it, turning the faceted elongate form in his hand and running a finger along its smooth surface.

'I will need you all to help me carry these to Nerthule, but first I will make a place for them there.' He grabbed a large handful and placed them inside pockets stitched into his robe. 'I will need these first.'

Ra climbed back up the ladder and returned to the Pool Stone. Eau hurried after him, eager to please. 'Shall we be taken in the storm that brought you here?' she said, her voice shaking.

'This will be so. But when I return to take you, you must all be silent upon reaching Nerthule. I do not wish the likes of you to disturb the inhabitants.'

The Astellite nodded weakly. 'Ra has spoken. It will be done,' Eau assured him.

The corners of his mouth rose in a snigger. 'Blessings of Ra upon you my sisters.'

Ra removed one of the crystals from a pocket and held it above his head where a ray from one of the crystal arrays struck it, causing the air to shudder and the storm to return. In moments, he was gone again.

* * *

The Yu-essence of the Yidrogh faugs had a bitter tang to it that was absent in the Faug Forest recipe. Mirrortac, Ameece and the triplets had a sip of it, but the hyfnuks did not partake.

'*Do you hear my thoughts,*' Mirrortac communicated to the triplets.
'*I hear you, dada!*' Treetam sent back.
'*And I you too, Treet,*' Mitac added.
'Hey, wow!' Ezof thought. '*It's just like we're talking to each other!*'

With some practice, they learned how to direct their telepathy to one or all five of them and exclude any private thoughts. Even Mirrortac found it easier after taking the essence than how it was before communicating with the roznoghs.

The next morning Treetam sought out the storage chamber where she had seen the helmets. There were many, but it was decided that the hyfnuks would stay behind, including Evarngar, who until this time had never left the side of his mistress as her protector. They agreed to guard the two combined Stones of Destiny – Oashu and Darm, and the Werdstone should anyone come snooping around the palace. The helmets were star-shaped like the crowns worn by the Astellites, and each found a size that fitted snugly, and laughed at how they looked in the bizarre headgear.
'I wonder what Nerthule is like,' Treetam mused. 'Does it have trees, and will the sky be blue like here?'
'Bluer,' Mirrortac answered.
'But how do you know that. You haven't gone there.'
'I have ... well, naught in body. It was a vision.'
'Dada! What did you see?' Treetam asked.
The others gave excited nods.
Mirrortac warmed to the telling. 'It was when I was in the pyramid on the island of Plumer-Ra. I was with the Ra-finelles when I was taken into a dream. Nerthule had such wonderness to behold. The endless lake was such a blue that reflected into the sky, and I could see many slups (fish) and creatures swimming. Some of them seemed to speak to me, but then all in Plumer-Ra spoke ... even the

trees,' he chuckled.

The elder erfin's smile suddenly disappeared as he thought about the visions that followed – the wars, the killing devices. He sighed and waved away any more questions. 'That is enough. We must prepare for our journey, then you will see for yourself little ones.'

Mitac gathered the solar-bites and gave them to the hyfnuks after instructing them in their use. He fell into Daghva's arms and hugged him, as he had found a friend in the hyfnuk who was always ready with sage advice about the dangers they could face. Evarngar held back tears as he farewelled the former Werdstone guardian whose life he held dear since she was just a child. He peered at her out of weepy dark brown eyes before addressing the erfin she held so dear.

'You must protect her now, erfin. If you should fail I will seek you out and tear you apart,' he warned, winking.

'You have guarded her well, Evarngar. I will die first before letting any harm come to my dearness.'

Evarngar allowed a hint of a smile. 'Then your life be forfeit, as mine was.'

He approached and opened his palm to reveal a dark crystal pendant. 'You will need this to speak back to us. I found it under the Werdstone pedestal.'

Ameece approached the tall hyfnuk and nuzzled him affectionately before resting her head against his chest. 'You are in my heart always. Know this!'

The triplets had finished saying their goodbyes to the hyfnuks, wiping tears from grey furry faces.

'To Nerthule and the Einuk stone!' Ezof announced, grinning through quivering lips.

Mirrortac glanced up at Evarngar. 'Be you ready?'

The hyfnuk mounted the steps to the pedestal and dialled in the symbol for Nerthule, but left his hand poised above the Werdstone.

'When you be prepared!' he said, looking up at the five.

They all stepped nervously towards the centre of the hall where a dais had risen from the floor. Mirrortac pulled Ameece up, then the triplets followed and linked hands in a close huddle.

'Be you ready?' he said, scanning the eyes of his family.

They nodded in silence.

Mirrortac caught Evarngar's eye. 'It is time.'

Evarngar's hand descended upon the Werdstone, which immediately activated. The five steeled themselves for the storm as the dais rumbled beneath them, and the vortex descended. They watched the surroundings become a blur as a dark spinning wall merged in around them. The darkness deepened until they could see nothing, which only made them cling more closely to each other as they felt their feet leave the floor. There was an instant feeling of nausea and motion. Then the nausea left, though the air around them tightened, constricting them like Mirrortac remembered of the suffocating thock tree of the Faug Forest. The feeling of compression continued while all their other senses were turned off. They were blind, deaf and dumb, shooting across the cosmos at incredible speed, twisting and turning in some wild ride that went on and on, sucking them through the tiniest of travelling holes until they felt they couldn't breathe or move a finger or a toe. They wanted to scream but their voices failed them.

After what seemed forever, they could no longer feel their bodies, and felt themselves floating. Stars and planets whizzed past; whole constellations took on a white fuzzy appearance. Spectres of beings flashed in front of them, lit up in an aura of entrancing coloured light. Some had a bearing of peace and calm while others scowled at them as they passed. The angry ones' auras were dark, flashing with angry reds and yellows, while the calm ones emanated indigo, green and blues; a few in bright golden hues.

However, they had little time to ponder on these visions, or were they merely dreams of unconscious minds? In what seemed like days, although time could not be measured, they saw a tiny blue dot emerge into a full-size planet before the blackness eddied all around again and feeling returned.

The floor was cool beneath their feet, but the air hot. The five found themselves in a jumble of bodies with their hands so tightly linked that each had to force their fingers apart. It was dark but as eyes adjusted, they could discern objects that were lit up. Mirrortac's ears gradually tuned in to a repeating sound that jarred the senses. He focused on a red light that was spinning on the dark ceiling. The repetitive sound was loud and annoying. He tried to stand but flopped down as his legs felt like jelly. The others were having similar problems, moaning and trying to find their voices. The chamber had a musty smell of stone and ageing things. Mirrortac felt like he had spent a long night partaking of merma-mead, the intoxicating refresher served up in the Faug Forest. His head felt thick and sore; his body like he had been trampled under a giant's feet. At last he could sit up and look around at the long chamber with the blaring noise pulsing through his head. There were several tables nearby with a litter of carved objects and vases. Near him was a large sarcophagus, its lid slightly ajar, while all of it was a dull gold in hue. His eyes drifted across to a display that was lit up on a nearby table. There was a large stone placed beneath a transparent case which was sealed all around its edges. He gathered all his strength and pulled himself up next to the table where he could see the stone clearly.

His lips curled with satisfaction.

The orange stone was curved on one side and roughly triangular, bearing a whirl design that pointed out from the curve. 'Einuk!' Mirrortac announced, shattering the silence with his rasping voice.

Ameece pulled herself up beside him while the others could rise without aid, still rubbing feeling into their limbs.

'Looks like Darm, only the colour is different,' Treetam said, reaching out her hand to touch the glass case enclosing it.

Mirrortac was about to try to move the case when they all heard a creaking sound, and a man's voice shouting at them.

'You! Step away from that!' A door to the room was ajar and framed within it was the silhouette of a man wearing something on his head.

Startled, the five turned as one towards the interloper. The man moved further into the room until he was illuminated under a small ceiling light.

'What ... who are you? Put your hands up where I can see them and don't try anything. I'm a crack shot!'

The Nerthulian was taller than them but slimmer in appearance. He wore a close-fitting garment with a soft cap on his head. He was holding what appeared to be a weapon with both hands, as though it were heavy. The barrel of the weapon was pointed at the group who were all holding their hands out from their sides.

'Up! Put your hands up in the air!'

They slowly complied, a little bemused at this ritual. Why such interest in their hands, and in the air no less?

The man was frowning as he took one hand off the weapon and reached across to a rectangular black object that was clipped to his shirt. He raised the object to his mouth and began to speak into it.

'Khalim here. I've got an interesting one for you. I've caught some thieves in animal costumes in the research lab. They were trying to pinch a rock in a case. Must be important or they wouldn't put it in a case, right.'

The rectangular box crackled, and a voice magically issued out of it.

'Got it Khalim. This I must see. Be right there.'

'Bring the others, Mikael. This is the strangest creepiest costumes I've ever seen.'

'Yes, we're coming ... over.'

Mirrortac tried to calm the man. 'Nerthulian, I am Mirrortac from Eol, and these three be my children. The she-one is Ameece. We must destroy this stone to save your world and ours.'

The man grimaced. 'You trying to say you are aliens? Then how is it you speak such fluent Arabic?'

'The essence makes us understand all tongues, and speak them,' Mirrortac said, but the man didn't look at all convinced.

'You will have to do better than that ... and just how did you get in here? I can't see any broken windows in the room.'

'A magic gateway ... ah ... portal,' Mitac interjected.

There was the sound of footsteps outside the room before three more men entered. They all had dark features while their hair had been trimmed neatly close to the head, and one had a black beard.

'Whew! Allah be praised,' the bearded man exclaimed. 'They look so real. The eyes ... how did you do that? Like those Hollywood creatures. Amazing!' The man ventured close to Treetam, reaching out to examine her fur and prod at her face.

Treetam winced and retreated a little as the man pinched her cheeks.

'Ow ... hands off Nerthule man!'

The bearded man grinned. 'A woman! Hmmm, are you naked under there? I will visit you in prison. But on second thought you may need a bath first; you smell like camel's dung.'

'They say they are aliens who came here through one of those ... you know ... wormhole things. Straight into the museum! Handy that ... and they think that rock over there is a danger to mankind.' Khalim laughed, and the other men joined in.

'Oh, by Allah, what a story!' the bearded one chortled. 'I must tell that to my children. Best one I have heard for stealing valuable museum artefacts ... dangerous!' The four men laughed again.

Treetam narrowed dagger eyes at the men. 'You think us amusing? That rock is one of the Stones of Destiny. It may look like a pretty thing, but it is what allowed us to come here. When Ra gains control of it, you will be his slaves.'

This only made the men laugh more; so much that tears were streaming out of their eyes and they were bent over in laughter.

'Ah, such play acting! I have never met such funny thieves,' the bearded man blurted between bursts of laughter.

Khalim was patting his chest trying to stop from laughing. 'If you want Ra, he is sleeping. He will come up again tomorrow.'

The other men burst into another bout of laughter.

'And why do you wear stars on your heads? You are star children, right?' Khalim laughed again.

The communicator crackled into life again. 'Yes, it is Khalim,' The man answered.

'You might like to take a look at the CCTV tape,' A nervous voice said. 'I don't think our thieves are exactly human.'

Khalim chuckled. 'Don't worry, Ahmed. They are in costume.'

'I am not so sure of that. Come and take a look,' Ahmed insisted.

'All right! For your sake ... but I think you read too many of those ghost stories.'

Khalim replaced the communicator and glanced around at the other men. 'Keep an eye on the "aliens". Ahmed wants me. He is wetting his pants.'

The men chuckled as Khalim left the room.

Mirrortac scrutinised the men smugly. 'The one you call Ahmed saw us appear from his crystal box. He believes that we are who we say we be.'

The bearded one grinned back. 'Crystal box? ... ah, the CCTV monitors. Very clever of you. You overheard Ahmed.'

'I entered Ahmed's mind as I can yours.'

The three men burst into laughter again before the bearded one stepped towards Mirrortac.

'Prove it then, alien. Tell me what I am thinking?'

Mirrortac and the others suddenly looked embarrassed.

The elder erfin bent his head towards the man and whispered. 'Be you certain that you wish the others to know of this?'

The bearded man looked uncertain for a moment before nodding. 'Yes. You could not possibly know what I am thinking. You're bluffing.'

'All right. If that be your wish,' he said as he turned to the other men. 'Your colleague here thinks of bedding a woman.'

The other men burst into guffaws while the bearded man's face paled.

'Argh ... all men think of bedding a beautiful woman.' He turned away with a dismissive wave.

The erfins and Ameece took the opportunity to remove their cumbersome headgear, placing the star-forms on the floor.

'Your friend Khalim is returning,' Mirrortac interrupted.

The other men teased the bearded one about what he was thinking when Khalim re-entered the room. He was frowning and muttering to himself before pulling the other men aside.

Mickael, one of the clean-faced men, whose skin was darker than the others, saw Khalim's expression. 'What is it, Khalim? You look as though Ramses II has risen from his coffin and appeared to you.'

Khalim glanced back at the erfins and Ameece before speaking to the men in soft tones. 'Unless one of you is playing a trick with the CCTV cameras, these ... whatever they are ... just came out of the air as from a desert wind.'

The bearded man tried to laugh it off. 'Argh, I cannot believe it! Of course, this must be a trick!'

It be no trick! Mirrortac's voice echoed in their minds.

The men paused, unsure that it wasn't their minds playing games.

Yeah, you all heard me. Foolish Nerthulians!

They exchanged bewildered glances. 'Di ... did you hear that? He's talking in our heads!' Khalim growled.

The others nodded slowly then began backing away from the furry visitors.

The bearded man was no longer amused. 'You cat things ... I don't know where you come from, but I must ask you not to touch anything in here, especially that stone.'

He turned to Khalim, stealing glances at Mirrortac and the others. 'What do we do? We have no protocol for this. There is nothing – no procedure – in the manual about handling real aliens … although I still think this is some elaborate hoax.'

Khalim stroked his chin for a moment. 'Yes, there is a procedure. Not exactly for aliens, but for anything of an international nature. And this is of an international nature. We must contact the General Intelligence Service. They will handle it. If it is some kind of hoax then … well, they will go to prison for a long time.'

The bearded one nodded. 'I will stay here with these aliens. You men guard outside the door, and Khalim can call the GIS.'

Mikael and the other man exited the room as Khalim turned to speak to the bearded man again.

'I will return once I have spoken with the GIS … if I can convince them! I can show them the tape, I suppose.'

Khalim turned on his heel and left in a loud clutter of footsteps as his boots echoed down the outer hall. The bearded man was serious now as he held up his weapon.

'I am but a lowly Egyptian and I do not care what you are. I will protect our ancient treasures, so do nothing to make me shoot you.'

Mirrortac sighed. 'As you see Nerthule man, we have no weapons.'

And why do you call me Nerthule man? What is "Nerthule", alien?'

'It be the name given to this world of yours. Therefore, you are Nerthulians.'

Nerthulians hey … I am an Egyptian, but there are many races of humans on this Earth.'

'So it is also on Mareos. I am an erfin and my she-one is a roznogh.'

'And these others … the small ones,' pointing at the triplets, 'Are they your children?'

Mirrortac nodded. 'They were born together.'

The bearded man and Mirrortac conversed about life on their two planets as though they were neighbours swapping gossip. The triplets and Ameece added their own contributions to the conversation until they all felt relatively relaxed. The alarm had stopped sounding but the security guard still did not trust them enough to lower his weapon. After some time, they heard a commotion in the halls and the sound of many men's voices. The bearded man's communicator crackled, and a stern voice issued.

'This is Ibrahim Nkosi of the GIS. We want you out of there now! You and the other guards will be quarantined.'

'Yes sir. But who will guard the … err aliens?'

'We have men coming in. Just go now!'

The bearded man made a gesture of respect towards the group before bowing.

Mirrortac bowed back as the man hurried out of the room while another entered dressed in a bulky suit that covered his whole body, leaving only a transparent square over the man's face. He was quickly followed by several others dressed the same, all carrying backpacks comprised of cylinders and joined to their suits with flexible hoses. The peculiar men could be heard breathing as they approached them. Without saying a word, they grabbed Mirrortac and the others and led them out of the room. They were marched through empty hallways and past displays of ancient artefacts while other men remained behind with machines that whined and sprayed the air with a disinfecting substance. When they reached the main hall, they saw that a fabric tunnel had been hastily installed through the main doorway between high pillars and down stairs into a large metal vehicle that stood on wheels. The air in the tunnel was cool and breezy, and soon the group, including the security guards, had been placed in the rear of the large vehicle before the tunnel was removed and the doors shut behind them.

Mirrortac and the others were not overly surprised when the vehicle rumbled into life and began moving. It wasn't a smooth motion like Wa-ku's craft, but uncomfortably unstable as the vehicle swayed and bumped along its route. The vehicle stopped after a time and another tunnel was connected to the doorway before they were again led out into a more sterile building with lower ceilings, and walls and floors made of unknown materials. The place was brilliantly illuminated from panels inset into the ceilings. They sniffed at the strange scents of the room that they entered, noting the presence of many devices and more men and women in white protective suits. A white-suited woman leaned towards one of the men who had brought them in and indicated Ezof. 'This one will do,' she said, without acknowledging them. They singled out Ezof and took him to the woman who revealed a syringe and injected Ezof with it. Mirrortac moved to stop her but two men held him.

'He will be all right. You understand?' The woman enunciated the words to the erfin.

Ezof began to breathe in a panic. 'What is happening? I feel so tired ...' He went limp and fainted but two of the men already were holding him up and dragging him towards a raised metal bed.

Mirrortac pulled against his captors while Ameece cried out and was herself prevented from coming to her son's aid. 'What are you doing to him? Did you kill him with that poisonous barb?'

A man stepped forward. 'Relax. We will not harm him. We have just put him to sleep.'

The men dragging Ezof then lifted him onto the bed before the woman instructed them to roll the bed to a large device at one end of the room.

The man who had earlier stepped forward now spoke again. 'If you are indeed from another planet, then we must take precautions not to be infected with some alien virus. Our scientists are also interested in you; and therefore, they will be making a few tests. There is nothing to worry about. Do not be alarmed.'

Mirrortac huffed in agitation. 'Virus? Scientists? I find this vexing.'

'Do you not get sick?' the man said in his deep mellow tones before he made a gesture of coughing by way of explanation.

Treetam, who had kept silent, raised an eyebrow. 'Ah ... the body demons.' Ameece and Mirrortac nodded in recognition.

The man shook his head. 'You are so advanced to be able to come here yet you have primitive ideas about disease.'

'We understand little, Nerthulian. It is the ones who command the Greater Sky who are "advanced" as you say.'

The woman with Ezof was operating the large device that slid of its own accord across the prostrate body of the young erfin. Another was taking samples of his blood, fur and other body fluids while an internal picture of Ezof's body was displayed on a screen near where the woman was controlling the scanner. This stunned them.

Treetam gasped. 'What sorcery sees through to the bones even when my brother be not dead?'

Ezof was wheeled away and the woman spoke directly to the group. 'We need not put you all to sleep if you will cooperate with our tests.'

Mitac edged forward. 'It does not hurt, right?'

'Just a little sting when we take a sample of your blood,' she assured.

Mitac looked back at Ameece with uncertainty.

'If you say you will naught cause injury,' Ameece said to the woman.

'You are perfectly safe.' The nurse proffered the bed that had been placed under the scanner.

Mitac walked over to the bed and lay down on it. The woman and her assistant repeated the same tests that had been done on Ezof. Treetam, Ameece and Mirrortac then followed until they had all been tested.

When Mirrortac stood up off the bed, Ezof was groaning to wakefulness. 'What happened,' he said as he sat up, and realising he was on a narrow bed, nearly fell off. 'How ...?' he muttered, jerking his head left and right.

'You will be all right,' the woman called out. 'It is natural to feel a little disoriented after recovering from the tranquilliser.'

Treetam smiled at her brother. 'Bro, you missed the "tests". We could see the bones through your body. Weird to the max.'

'Too right. Glad to see you back,' Mitac said.

'I don't understand. How can you see my bones?' Ezof rubbed his forehead.

'They have a magic box that shows what is inside you,' Treetam replied.

'Well, it may seem like magic to you,' the head man interjected. 'These are all machines that our science and technology has created,' he explained.

'I should like to learn of this science and technology,' Mitac said as he examined the devices and equipment in the room.

Mitac pulled at his brother's arm. 'Come Ezof. Let me show you the bone-looker.'

Ezof brightened as Mitac approached the scanner and put his arm under it. He pressed a button with his other hand and waited for the device to spring into life.

'Um, don't touch that,' one of the scientists shouted.

The device made a humming sound as a metal instrument slid across Mitac's arm. The scientist hastened towards him to stop him, but another of the men raised up a palm to forestall him.

Ezof gasped in awe as an image of Mitac's arm bones appeared on a screen alongside the device. 'I can see your bones! I can see your bones!' he uttered.

The scientists' hooded faces grinned at his reaction. The woman patted Mitac on the shoulder. 'You're a fast learner. You would be a good scientist,' she said.

Mirrortac grimaced. 'We are wasting time. Now you have done your tests, we wish to return to the stone in the temple of aged things ... the museum,' he said.

The head man bowed to Mirrortac. 'I am sorry. The stone you speak of is precious to us at this time. We must examine it, and we must know why you would travel from a planet far far away for a stone that has been lying in a sarcophagus at the bottom of the Mediterranean Sea for thousands of years. But before you answer that and our other questions, we must move you to a quarantine facility.'

'But the stone is dangerous! It must be destroyed ... and the two other Stones of Destiny.'

Mirrortac began to pace back and forth.

'All in good time,' the man said all too politely. 'I am not the one who will speak to you about this matter. Someone will speak to you in the morning about it. Now if you would care to come with us,' he indicated the doorway to the hall. 'It has been a long night.'

The erfin sighed. 'Come family.'

They returned through the hallway and into the back of the vehicle, but the security guards were no longer with them. They had been taken to another room in the complex and cleansed of any possible contaminants. The erfins could not see out as the vehicle made its way again through a circuitous route until coming to a stop in front of a large building where they were led to a sparse room with bedding and a transparent wall that saw through to an adjacent room with seating. Dim lighting was sufficient to allow them to move around without bumping blindly into anything. The door to the room was secured after they were told to sleep until sunrise.

Ameece nuzzled up against Mirrortac's chest as they shared a bed. 'We must be patient with the Nerthulians,' she said softly. 'They have strange ways and much powerful magic, but I see no malice in their hearts.'

Mirrortac rested his head on the fluffy fabric. 'I fear their curiosity is extreme. They even want to know about our bodies and what is inside of us.'

'I do find that difficult to understand. What benefit is it to know such things?' she said.

He let out a long breath. 'We cannot move the stone until Wa-ku returns in any case. We must use the talking stone to tell Evarngar and the others what has happened.'

Ameece removed the pendant from around her neck and stroked it as she had the Werdstone. The stone flickered with a dull green light before fading back to its original dark composition. She tried again but the light was weak.

'Evarngar!' she said into the stone. 'Evarngar!' she repeated.

The stone made a barely audible crackle before fading again.

She frowned at it. 'I should have used it while we were near the Einuk stone. We are too far from it now to use it anymore.'

'Then there be no more we can do now. We must sleep,' Mirrortac said.

* * *

They awoke to find platters of beans, bitter vegetables and a yellow processed substance had been placed on a table in the room. There were also mugs filled with juiced fruit that they all found refreshing. When they had finished eating and had been given time to tend to their toiletry in the adjacent anteroom, the man calling himself Ibrahim Nkosi entered with another man whose skin was paler. Ibrahim was clean shaven with brown skin and eyes while the other man had short silvan hair and grey eyes, and he too was clean shaven. They both sat down facing the transparent wall and detached two speaking and hearing devices from the wall. The devices fitted neatly over their heads, leaving their hands free.

Mirrortac and Ameece approached the wall as Ibrahim waved them forward and pointed to identical headsets on the quarantine room side. They timidly placed the headsets on but were having difficulty as their heads were wider than that of the Nerthulians, and their ears stuck up rather than from the side of their heads.

'Can you hear me,' Ibrahim asked, and the two nodded.

'Speak into the mouthpiece ... I need to know that I can also hear you.'

'I am here ... Mirrortac,' the erfin ventured.

Both men smiled.

'As representative of the Egyptian republic, I welcome you all to our country and the world,' Ibrahim began.

'The president wishes to extend apologies for any discomfort you are enduring in staying in our quarantine facility. However, this is a necessary precaution ... and I am afraid that we will need to keep you in quarantine for another three weeks ... um that is 21 days if you understand. The tests of your body fluids have found bacteria not known on this Earth, and it will require the three weeks to replace these with Earth microbes. You will all be washed clean of exterior pathogens and transferred into a more comfortable quarantine facility to allow you more room to move around.'

'That is many days to sit while Ra has use of the stone to enslave all of Nerthule,' Mirrortac growled. 'You are all so afraid on this world.'

Ibrahim looked down for a moment before raising his eyes again. 'That is true. But that is the way of this world.'

Ameece frowned. 'Be there any way that you can guard the stone ... put it somewhere that offers no escape for Ra when he returns through the portal.'

'We are considering our options, but no decision has been made about this stone. We are still studying it to see how such a thing can create a passage through space,' Ibrahim said.

'And that is why I have brought my colleague here who is from Australia ... another country a long way from us. He is an astrobiologist working with all the secret service agencies of the world in the field of life on other planets. Please let me introduce you to James Kelly.' The silvan haired man inclined his head in a short bow.

Mirrortac and Ameece returned the bow.

Kelly grinned widely. 'You're a sight for sore eyes people. What do you call yourselves? I don't want to be calling you furry person one and furry person two.'

Mirrortac introduced themselves but he could barely conceal his impatience as the questioning began.

'Erfins 'ay! We always visualised aliens as all the same, you know ... oval black eyes and skinny buggers with big heads. It's an eye-opener, I tell ya, to see aliens like you with lots of fur and all. If you excuse me saying, you're more like some of the creatures we have around here ... a bit of a cross between big cats and bears. But I suppose you don't have anything like that on your planet,' he said, then answered his own question. 'Nah ... I don't expect so. Look, what we want to know is what kind of life you have on your planet. Can you tell me what types of animals and people live on ... what's your planet called ...?'

'Mareos,' Mirrortac replied.

'Yeah, Mareos. And do you have plants there and that kind of thing?'

Mirrortac clenched his teeth but decided to answer as he had been used to doing in some way to all the peoples he had encountered in the different lands of his home world.

It was well into the latter part of the day when the sun outside was already setting that the incessant questioning finally came to an end. Mirrortac and Ameece had both grown tired of speaking and had called in the triplets to help them explain some of the things about Mareos that Kelly was keen to know. Mitac took great interest in what Kelly had to say about Nerthule and the discipline called science. Ibrahim had long since left the room to tend to other matters, and only returned when Kelly had called him on his communication device he called a cell phone.

Ibrahim put on the headset and noticed how Mirrortac rolled his eyes.

'It has been a long day, I know. There will be no more questions for now, but there has been a change in plan. We wanted you to enjoy the hospitality of our Egypt a little while longer but, alas, our hands have been tied, so to speak … it is an expression to say that greater powers have overruled us, and we must cede to their wishes. You will be moved to a quarantine facility in Switzerland … and, of course, all protective measures will be used in your transport.'

Mirrortac removed his headset and rubbed his sore ears. He had heard enough for the day and this was another frustrating development. Ameece nuzzled him and kept her composure.

The elder erfin snarled. 'This will take us further from the stone. These Nerthulians are impossible! Do they not want to be saved from enslavement? They remind me of the talkative Petros … so much chatter and little to show for it!'

Ezof pouted. 'I wish I had one of those solar–bites now. Just blast our way out of here and go get that stone.'

Mitac commiserated. 'With all the magical things they own, I imagine the Nerthulians will soon kill us or something worse.'

'Mitac is right bro. We can't fight these Nerthulians … not, at least, until we know how to outwit them,' Treetam said.

The white cloaked people soon arrived to lead them again through the tunnel and into another vehicle. Then onward they drove until they were transferred to a larger vehicle with rigid wings. Several large guards accompanied them and were seated beside each one on soft couches. The small windows were covered, blocking any view of the world itself, which they had yet to glimpse. There was a soft whine as the craft taxied along the smooth surface, then a roar and an enormous force as it was propelled forward and assumed into the air. While much smoother than that of the ground vehicle, this one sometimes shuddered, rose and fell with a giddy motion. The alien guests were treated to a dinner of prepared food that had been heated. Mirrortac recognised that he was eating some kind of meat, but it was no longer raw and had a mixture of flavours blended into it. He didn't have to chew as much as the meat just fell apart in his mouth as though it was as soft as fruit.

'What have you done to this flesh?' he asked the guard beside him. 'It is hot and lacks toughness.'

'We cook it. To keep the bacteria out … no disease,' the man stated.

'Fear governs your lives it seems,' Mirrortac remarked.

The man only gave a polite smile behind the window of his hood. Another of the men was fidgeting in a seat towards the front of the plane. He referred often to a device on his cloaked wrist before slipping up the shade on his window and looking out. Another man opposite him looked across to the man briefly before checking a similar device on his own wrist.

Treetam rested her head on her adopted mother and went to sleep. Ezof talked to Mitac about acquiring a bow, and Mitac agreed that he had missed the primitive weapon since leaving the Faug Forest.

Mirrortac tried to tune into the minds of the men, and it was the fidgety man who gained his attention.

'*Just another two minutes … inject the Egyptians then the plane's ours.*'

The erfin wondered about what the man meant by 'minutes', 'inject'and 'plane'. It sounded suspicious. He decided to ask him.

'*What are minutes Nerthule man?*' he directed.

The man appeared startled and glanced around then straight at the erfin.

'*Did you just talk inside my head, alien?*'

'*It is I who speaks,*' the erfin replied.

'*Unreal! Minutes … it is a time measurement. A minute is a count of 60.*'

'*And inject? You wish to inject the Egyptians?*' Mirrortac pressed on.

The man paled but kept his composure. '*You are going to have to trust me, alien. I cannot explain now, but you will see soon enough.*'

At that the man consulted his watch again then looked across at the other across the way. The other man glanced back and gave a barely perceptible nod before standing up. Then the first man was up as well, and both were moving towards the erfins and the guards seated beside them.

'What are you doing?' the man beside Mirrortac asked, annoyed.

'Taking care of business,' the first man answered.

The two guards beside the erfins were about to draw their weapons when the two men lunged at them, revealing syringes and plunging them into the guards' sides before they had a chance to react. The guards both tried to retaliate but were rapidly overcome by the drug, slumping down and flopping out of their seats.

The first man peered at Mirrortac through his hood. 'Sorry to do this, guys. We are taking you to the land of the free, America. I'm sure our people will be most interested in your telepathic ability. I will be giving the pilot his new heading, but we'll have to make a quick stop to refuel. It's quite a-ways.'

THE ARREST

Members of the Uranian guard escorted Yidu along the long hallway that constituted the main artery of the Halls of Ra. The duoculi (two-eyed) guards were robed in black silk with hair closely cropped to the head. Yidu did not struggle but strode with his head held high, betraying no emotion. A burnt scar in the centre of his forehead was all that was left of his third eye. His hands were secured behind his back with manacles. His duoculi brother trailed behind in his anti-gravity chair, his simple green robe no match for Yidu's glistening garment that was like a moving rainbow as he walked. Wa-ku operated his chair over a line of metal that was inlaid into the floor, enabling the chair to hover above it. A line of guards stood on either side of the hallway, astride rows of marble columns. The ceiling high above was crystalline in structure and neatly webbed in hexagonal patterns throughout. The curved arc of the ceiling met bleached stone halfway down the walls where elongated crystal insets glowed with a suffused yet bright light that illuminated the entire hallway. At the end of the hallway were the huge ebony timber doors of the main chamber where the open council met four times a year, and beside it at right was a smaller doorway – the Chamber of the Inner Council where judicial matters were handled.

Two more duoculi guards stood at either side of the entrance to the Chamber of the Inner Council and moved in with the guards taking Yidu as they entered the chamber. Facing them was a semi-circular stone table with ten moulded seats, and a satin blue drape fell from the ceiling to the floor behind. A triangle pattern was etched into the centre of the drape, and inside the triangle was an eye connected with curved lines to two sides of the triangle and surrounded by three stars near each corner. The men took their place before a row of benched seating as the members of the inner council made their way into the chamber from a side door. Five duoculi and five tresoculi took their seats, and the guards bowed deeply before they all sat down. One of the duoculi – a man with long grey hair falling over his shoulders, and blue eyes, scrutinised the men before speaking.

'We are here to consider a case against one Yidu, given the keeping of Mareos, Thenigmas and Nerthule, on a charge of intent to enslave and usurp absolute rule through the misuse of the knowledge of the Ancients as communicated through the sacred Werdstone. It is alleged the one Yidu also sought to gain this absolute command through the alignment of the Three Stones of Destiny – Oashu, Darm and Einuk. What say you Yidu in defence of these charges?'

Yidu stared up smugly. 'It is all in the Game, honoured one. I am merely doing as many others have done ... but succeeding. This brother of mine is a hypocrite. He too enslaved the Petros and was undone by the same meddling furball that dare destroy all my hard work. If you wish to bring this charge upon me, then my brother Wa-ku must also be included.'

The grey-haired man set his gaze on Yidu. 'The accused cannot set a charge against another. The one Wa-ku has withdrawn from his error, although it is not he who has charge over the Werdstone or the Three Stones of Destiny. Your charge is by far the more serious, as you have broken a sacred trust. Do you deny it?'

Yidu went to stand up but was restrained. 'Your days are ending, old man. The tresoculi will rise again to take their rightful place and will finish what we started so long ago!'

An angry murmur rose among the members of the inner council, and the grey-haired representative snarled back at Yidu. 'This is insolence! You dare challenge the council with words of treason! You stand betrayed by your own pride. Of what conspiracy do you pretend to know? You are an offence and embarrassment to your tresoculi brethren who sit here before you.'

Yidu just smiled at this. 'You will know soon enough with the new resurrection of Ra, the great and rightful master of Nerthule. You will see the rise of a new Atlantis, and no-one will be able to stop him.'

There were gasps among the assembled as the chairman rose stunned. 'What do you know about this, Wa-ku? Surely this is a lie. Ra is believed dead when the quake sunk the city. How can this be?'

Wa-ku pushed himself up on his hoverchair. 'There are witnesses who saw the image of Ra appear in Yidu's palace in Skye, and swear he wore the golden robe and the sun-plate as the Werdstone portal was activated.'

'And who be these witnesses?' the chairman enquired.

'They were the erfins Mirrortac and three of his kin, and the roznogh Ameece.They are the same who defeated Yidu's dragon.'

'Amazing, that mere erfins and roznoghs can defeat such a one. How is that possible?'

'I did give them some assistance, honoured one. They used the solar-bites, and a little of their own magic.'

The chairman stroked his chin and leaned forward. 'Magic, you say. Who set them upon such a path? It is nigh impossible to enter and cross Skye with all the constructs that Yidu set up.'

Wa-ku nodded. 'Indeed, honoured one. I believe the erfin Mirrortac is no ordinary erfin. This is his second mission set by some agent we do not know, but I suspect from beyond the worlds. Yidu did send him to Thenigmas where he lost all memory of who he was or his mission. It was only through the intercession of his three brave children and a little help from myself that he was able to complete his mission.'

'Do not tell me that this Mirrortac is now intending to engage Ra. While Yidu proved impossible, if Ra is allowed to ascend to power again, no-one will be able to challenge him.'

Wa-ku's head dropped in a heavy sigh. 'He is intent on gathering the last of the Three Stones of Destiny and destroying it. At this moment, he and his kin are on Nerthule.'

The chairman looked back at him incredulous, then turned to the others of the council. There was hushed muttering as the ten engaged in discussion for some time, a few occasionally glancing back at Yidu and Wa-ku. Finally, the chairman looked up and addressed them.

'Guards, stand at the doors. This is an emergency alert, you understand. We are going into private session.'

The door guards immediately stepped back and withdrew to the entrance which they bolted shut. The other guards opened a slat in the floor before Yidu and withdrew large chains that they clamped to the tresoculi's ankles and secured through the floor slat. The council members rose and left the room through their own side door.

Yidu laughed as they left. 'It has begun! Ra the great one, shining sun, our travesty is undone!'

Wa-ku glared at his brother. 'What is begun will be the only thing undone. I am ashamed to call you kin.'

'As if I care. I will be free once the revolution starts.'

'Huh! The only revolution is in your head. You will rot in solitary.'

The brothers continued to curse each other and argue until the council again emerged from their session and took their seats once more.

This time it was a bearded tresoculi member who spoke.

'I and my colleagues are ashamed to call this one Yidu a tresoculi and Uranian. We have agreed to banish him to the dark quadrant to spend the rest of his days alone with the fire creatures.'

Yidu pulled at his chains and began struggling with the guards restraining him. 'No! You cannot do this. You are the traitors ...'

'Silence prisoner!' The chairman shouted.

'I will not be silenced you poor excuse for a Uranian!' Yidu cut in.

The chairman's face turned red with rage. 'How dare you! Take the prisoner away!'

The guards unlocked the link to the floor and manhandled Yidu as he continued to struggle against them. The door guards unbolted the door and helped the others drag Yidu back into the hallway. He was still shouting and cursing the council as they took him down the hall.

The chairman motioned for Wa-ku to stay. 'We did not realise that the erfin Mirrortac has set on gathering the Three Stones of Destiny to destroy them. It astounds us that he knows that this is the only way to stop Yidu, and now Ra. But he and his kin will fail if we do not step in to assist. The news of Ra's return is most distressing and of cosmological import. We have decided to convene an emergency meeting of the entire Council of Atlantis to discuss our intervention as Ra will be almost impossible to defeat once he has gained the power of the alignment of the three planets. Even with one of the stones removed from Thenigmas, the alignment between Mareos and Nerthule will be intense. It will take some time to alert the entire council membership of 100 provinces, but we must act in haste, as every day lost is one closer to alignment for Ra.'

Wa-ku could see the lines of anxiety on the old man's face and that of his colleagues. He thought of the naivety of Mirrortac in his quest but had to admit he had succeeded beyond all expectations to bring Yidu to heel. The erfin had realised that Yidu's power to uphold the dragon transformation was in his third eye, and by having Mitac destroy it with a beam from the solar-bite weapon was pure genius. Once the dragon's third eye was blinded, the whole dragon construct fell to pieces, leaving only the weakened man. Wa-ku thought that was finally the end of it, and Yidu's rantings as he returned him to Kosmo were just a desperate attempt to tease and unhinge him.

He bowed to the council as his leave was granted, flicking the knob to operate his chair. Wa-ku had little memory of Ra who was a great uncle of he and Yidu. He last saw him thousands of years ago, but of course, it had only been fewer than 100 years with the help of the time suspension elements of galactic travel. He didn't quite understand it himself, but it all had to do with travelling at or near the speed of light. It was said that one could not travel faster than light, as the soul would then become separated from the body. The man shuddered as he contemplated the mysteries of the beyond, but that was something only the Ancients truly understood.

AN APPOINTMENT

The newly appointed curator in the New Kingdom section of the Egyptian Museum of Antiquities in Cairo was a tall man with sharp brown eyes and a turban wrapped around his head to halfway down his forehead and decorated at its centre with an oval glazed stone that was as dark as his eyes. He chose to wear a white robe – a galabeya – with red filigree patterns descending from the neck. Raul Haru had impressed the director of the museum with his knowledge concerning the New Kingdom period, and he was placed on special assignment to study the mysterious stone that was found with the sarcophagus discovered among the ruins of an ancient city at the bottom of the Mediterranean Sea. Raul was intrigued by the stone that had stumped the experts as to its origin. He said he would need some time to inspect the stone more closely, and its association with what was claimed to be a wormhole link to another planet purported to exist in the constellation of Orion. His ever-present companion was the astrobiologist James Kelly who was more interested in the stone's link to Mareos.

'That stone reminds me of our Aboriginal art. They made squiggles like that and used ochre colour from orange stones just like this one,' Kelly remarked.

'Maybe your indigenous people travelled in space thousands of years ago, or were visited by such a one,' Raul offered while not shifting his attention from the stone, which he inspected under an electron microscope to determine composition.

Kelly beamed. 'Yeah, could be. I have often thought that our Aborigines got a visit from aliens. Some of their cave paintings suggested beings with helmets. But then a lot of these religions talk of space beings and craft that came out of the clouds.'

Raul shifted his eyes to regard the two guards standing at the laboratory door before he adjusted the microscope's lens to another part of the curved stone.

'You have met the aliens who travelled here, I believe, Mister Kelly.'

'What makes you say that?' Kelly queried. 'Don't think you've been cleared, mate.'

Raul's eyes met Kelly's, and he spoke in soft measured tones. 'Of course, I am cleared, Mr Kelly. Mr Nkosi himself told me of the furry aliens who appeared here. How many were there ...' He looked up thoughtfully.

'Five ... there were five,' Kelly answered. 'You must have been cleared. Funny, Nkosi didn't mention it to me.'

Raul inspected the screen view of the stone's surface. 'Five, yes. You spoke to them, Mr Kelly?'

Kelly ran his fingers through his grey hair and looked back uncertainly. 'I think I've said enough for now.'

Raul's interest in the stone piqued. 'Hmmm. What is this?'

The Australian leaned in close to the screen where Raul was inspecting the whorl pattern. 'You found something, mate?'

'The pattern has a perfect edge. One could not paint with such exactness, though the Egyptian artisans were certainly adept ... just not quite this adept.'

Raul reached into his robe and pulled out a faceted stone that he offered to Kelly.

The Australian looked at the stone quizzically. 'What's this, mate?'

Raul gazed directly into Kelly's eyes. 'A gift. I feel I have over-stepped the mark and wish to offer this as recompense.'

Kelly waved his hands in dismissal. 'No, mate. It's all right. I'm not much for bling and gems. You keep it.'

'This is a rare gemstone, Mr Kelly. Our people believe it bestows protection upon the user. It is an offering of friendship and is ill-regarded if refused.'

Kelly reached out to the outstretched hand and picked up the stone. 'Well, put it that way. I'll treasure it.'

He was about to put the stone into his own pocket when the curator forestalled him.

'No. Do not put it away. Place it under your neck ... as you would a necklace.'

Kelly hesitated, his hand frozen in awkward transit to his pocket.

'Like I said, I'm not one for wearing jewellery.'

Raul grabbed Kelly's hand and gently pushed it towards his neck. 'Do not think of it as jewellery, my friend. This is more than mere adornment. Please, indulge me.'

'But it hasn't got any chain. How am I expected to wear it?'

Raul continued to gently push the stone towards Kelly's neck. 'Indulge me, Mr Kelly. Believe me, no chain is needed.'

Kelly reluctantly moved the stone towards his neck, only to be startled when it abruptly clung to the flesh below his throat without aid. In a second it had embedded itself.

Kelly shook his head for a moment then bowed with reverence. 'Peace upon you and your house, oh master.'

Raul let out a long breath. 'At last, enough of your country's colloquial expressions, Mr Kelly. You are now my subject. Now, tell me more of these aliens you met.'

* * *

The erfins hardly had a chance to stretch their legs after the plane landed on American soil before they were again hustled along through the familiar quarantine tunnel into a waiting van. This time they were afforded comfortable seating and windows that were not shielded, but only allowed them to look out and no-one to look in. Outside, the windows were a dark tint that appeared opaque while inside afforded a clear polarised view. The triplets eagerly crowded around the nearest window to peek out at a steel and concrete landscape. They could see thousands of people walking along the sides of wide roadways cluttered with vehicles both small and large. Buildings rose like metal mountains, affording only glimpses of blue sky. Mitac was especially intrigued at the vehicles that drove without any visible aid, and the coloured lights that shone out from buildings, spelling out strange names.

They were taken out of the city and along expansive pathways that were suspended above other roadways and swept out into a landscape of numerous dwellings of varying hues and design. In time the dwellings grew fewer, replaced by the vegetation of the land – trees, shrubs, large cropped fields kept in orderly fashion. In some places were creatures grazing, and even these were controlled much like the poultry fote of the erfins' homeland Eol. Eventually the ordered landscape became more chaotic and wilder as they climbed towards a low mountain range with little vegetation.

A gateway and a high metal wired fence formed a barrier where the vehicle stopped momentarily before the gate magically opened to allow their passage. They rounded a low hill, casting up dust into the air before entering an artificial cave where a steel wall closed in behind them.

Mirrortac was the first to alight. Nerthulians in quarantine suits opened the doors and led them into a tiled room where they were told to enter through a stream of water jets and bubbly fluid that soaked their bodies and lightly stung their skin. These were followed with another set of water jets and finally warm blasts of air that quickly dried their fur.

'Ooh, that is tingly,' Treetam remarked before sniffing at her clean fur. 'And its scent is like the blooms of the Yu-tree.'

Ameece smiled at her. 'Indeed, the Nerthulians have turned us into sweet-smelling things. It be pleasantly reassuring.'

Mirrortac grunted as he limped along the hallway with the guards who, for the first time since the museum, wore regular clothing except for breathing masks.

'Sweet smelling we may be, but all I can think of now is the Einuk stone now beyond our reach.'

Ameece hugged him in sympathy. 'Have you not learned patience my he-one. After your tales of the Petros, I would think you would need no more an example.'

The elder erfin sighed. 'I have grown weary … but time is no friend as Ra prepares to enslave all.'

The guards bid them enter through a doorway into a room where a distinguished group of men and women sat at table. A woman rose to greet them, offering a gloved hand to Mirrortac. Her hair was dark and cut short and her eyes tinged a light shade of brown. A transparent mask covered thick lips and shining white teeth. She kept her hand extended to the erfin before she blushed.

'Oh, I am sorry. It is our custom on this planet to extend a hand to each other in greeting. Just accept my hand and shake it up and down.'

Mirrortac inclined his head as he slowly offered his right hand and took her hand in his. He began to rigorously shake her hand which felt small and weak in his.

'Not so hard!' she blushed again. 'You only need a light shake … like this' and she demonstrated by moving his hand up and down.

The woman smiled, exposing perfect teeth. 'My name is Danielle King. I am a senior adviser to the President of the United States of America who is the leader of this country and in world affairs. We apologise for bringing you halfway around the world, but we feel we are best placed to enter into dialogue with cosmic races such as yourselves. We will make you as comfortable as possible but at this time must observe quarantine to ensure you do not inadvertently pass on any pathogens to the people and the flora and fauna of the Earth …'

'… and your name is?'

The erfin bowed. 'Mirrortac. This be my kin Ameece, Ezof, Mitac and Treetam.'

King shook all their hands and offered them seating before introducing the three people with her.

After all the introductions, servants entered bearing ceramic dishes of fruit and light pastries that the erfins ate with abandon, littering the floor around them with crumbs and seeds.

A large screen was revealed behind the advisers with an image of the planet and its land masses surrounded by massive ocean expanses.

King began to explain about the different countries and the Nerthulian customs, which were vast and seemingly endless in variety, before passing on to a secret service man who began questioning them on how and why they had come to Earth. When the Einuk stone was discussed, the man began questioning another woman with him before turning his attention back to Mirrortac.

'We need to bring that stone here, but the Egyptian authorities won't release it. They say they have to study it further,' the man said.

Mirrortac's eyebrows lifted. 'It is most important that this stone comes to us. The future of your planet depends on it,' he said, leaning over the table and clasping his fists.

'You say this is a matter of international security?' the man queried.

'The security of all the worlds depends on it,' Mirrortac stressed.

'Then the President will hear of it. He can demand that the Egyptian authorities release this Einuk stone.'

The elder erfin looked relieved. 'Sense at last.'

AN UPRISING

Seven days after calling for an emergency meeting of the full Council of Atlantis, the great ebony doors swung open as representatives of the 100 provinces paraded in to the main chamber where seating was arranged in several semicircles rising in levels facing the supreme chair. Wa-ku joined a representative for his province at the appropriate desk tagged with the name of the province. A voice amplification crystal was placed at each desk to allow for comment and discussion. An aged woman duoculi examined notes on a screen in front of her at the supreme chair's desk as provincial representatives found their seats. Green dewdrop gemstones hung from intricate clasps from her earlobes, and her fingers were adorned in gold rings clustered with gemstones and crystals. Her eyes were still a bright blue despite the wrinkles in her face and the white shock of hair that hung to one shoulder. The other side of her head was shaved and inscribed with symbols and she wore a green robe tied at the waist with a red belt.

'Hurry up people!' Her rasping voice shattered the murmur of idle chatter as many stopped to greet colleagues not seen in some time.

'Find your seats. We have serious business to discuss!'

Robed representatives cut short their greetings to bow to the chair as they hastened to their places.

The old woman's keen eyes watched them settle into their seats before ordering guards to shut the doors. Then, raising a green crystal staff, she surveyed the assemblage.

'In the name of the Ancient Werd, I convene this emergency session of the Council of Atlantis. Oh, great and holy be the Werd!' she proclaimed.

All the assembled bowed before answering in chorus. 'Great and holy be the Werd!'

Wa-ku leaned in to his provincial representative. 'Who is that?' he whispered.

'That's Maru. She descends from the Ancients and is said to be an actual 3000 years in age.'

'Whoa! I thought there was no-one left from the Ancients,' Wa-ku said.

The duoculi woman shook her head. 'There are not … at least not officially.'

Wa-ku could tell that the representative was secretive and did not wish to elaborate further.

Maru seemed to look up at him momentarily and smile before shifting her gaze.

'We are about to enter dark times,' the old woman announced, her face now set.

'I have been called upon to discern this rumour of Ra's rise from the bottom of the depths of the sea in Nerthule. And I am here to tell you that it is no rumour. Ra is indeed resurrected through the artifice of his own construction and is preparing to use the alignment to empower and enslave first in Nerthule and then in Mareos and Thenigmas … and then to corrupt the cosmological order.'

A murmur rose from around the chamber accompanied by stunned glances.

Maru waited a few moments until the exchange died down before speaking again. 'Yidu is part of the betrayal that as yet is to be revealed at its greatest extent. It is a plan hatched in his youth along with his co-conspirator and great uncle, Ra, who has lain asleep all this time since the sinking of Atlantis.'

A tresoculi member rose from his place. 'How do you know all this, aged one? Is it not just the deranged vision of some lowly furry ones?'

Maru met his eyes without flinching. 'I know because I have looked into the Pool of Knowledge. It is the truth that turns bitter in your mouth.'

The man grunted angrily. 'Only the Ancients can look upon the pool …'

'Precisely,' she said before he could say anything more.

Wa-ku could hear several gasps and a sudden hush fell on the chamber. The tresoculi member sat down stunned.

'And so should your face pale, Seth. I am the last. And it pains me to say that death will come to many before the alignment has ended. The "furry ones" as you call them are honourable erfins and a roznogh who share the same ancestry. They have a mission from beyond the Veil.'

There were more hushed murmurings throughout the chamber as Maru scrutinised the assemblage.

The woman with Wa-ku rose to signal her intention to speak, and Maru nodded her assent.

'Oh, great and honourable Maru. What do you propose we do?'

'It is imperative that we assemble all our fleet to foil Ra's plan. The erfins can only remove the Einuk stone but we must take Ra and his forces.'

'Forces? What forces oh honourable Maru?' another shouted from across the chamber.

'Ra has no forces yet, but when our ships arrive there, he will have amassed a great army that will yield to his every command.'

The member ran his fingers through his blond curls. 'But how can he achieve such a thing?'

Maru sighed. 'He will ... and he is. He has corrupted the shadow crystals to mesmerise anyone; and he has power to summon those who have slept for millennia.'

A jumble of voices competed for answers as the chamber erupted in consternation. Maru chose a duoculi who was standing at the back.

'Honourable Maru, what do you speak of? Are there more of the dead who will rise?'

The old woman inclined her head. 'They will seem like the dead rising, but they have been asleep as Ra has been asleep. They are not of Nerthule but of Thenigmas and Mareos and will be counted in their legion.'

Wa-ku caught sight of some movement in the chamber behind where Maru was addressing them. He blinked to confirm that something, or someone, had moved behind a column. Perhaps he was tired, he thought, or a servant had come to bring refreshments but did not wish to interrupt proceedings. Around him many of the members had left their places to confer with others. Maru looked up and shivered for a moment.

'The enemy is in our midst!' she warned. 'There is one more crucial news that I must tell you all ... to warn you.'

A shape emerged from behind the column behind her and raised what looked like a flute to its invisible face.

Wa-ku pushed himself up from his hoverchair. 'Maru! Behind you!'

His warning was too late. The old woman shuddered and stumbled, gasping for breath. A dark robed figure fled through an unseen opening before anyone could react. Maru collapsed in a heap on the tiled floor. Those nearest to her rushed to her side as she lay on the floor unconscious. Wa-ku jostled through the frightened crowd while someone raised the alarm, and soon a side door opened to blue robed medical attendants who made a swift passage to inspect the Ancient. Wa-ku finally made his way to where a group had gathered around the collapsed woman.

'Make space. Let us do our work,' an attendant growled.

Another was examining Maru and taking readings of her vitals.

'Is she dead? What happened?' someone said.

'I don't know. She just suddenly fell down,' another offered.

'It was an assassin,' Wa-ku spoke up.

'An assassin? Who would do this? Why?' a woman's voice said.

Wa-ku swallowed hard. 'Someone wants to shut her up,' he said.

The older attendant looked up at Wa-ku. 'She is not dead, but she has been paralysed by something poisonous. We must get her to the ward immediately. There are marks on her neck from a dart that must be on the floor here somewhere.'

'Found it!' a voice called out, and a tresoculi member stepped forward with a small dart. The attendant accepted it and placed it in a small tube which he stoppered and placed in the pocket of his robe. He then rummaged around in the medical kit to remove three large red crystals that he placed under Maru's back and head.

The Ancient began to levitate up from the floor, allowing the attendants to propel her through the side door and away to the wards in another building some blocks away. Meanwhile guards entered and locked all entrances and exits, leaving the representatives imprisoned in the main council chamber. The duoculi committee chairman who had called the meeting in the first place now entered before the last door was locked, accompanied by a team of military guards. He quickly moved up to the podium and took the crystal microphone.

'Return to your places all of you. I have placed the entire halls in lockdown. We have a traitor among us who wishes to silence the great and Ancient Maru. Please take out all the items you have on your person and place them on your desk. An inspection will be undertaken shortly.'

There was a clatter of objects being placed on desks as side doors opened. Soldiers and military officers filed into the chamber and lined up along the walls of the chamber until they made up the entire circumference. All of them were armed with solar-bites and stood resolute and expressionless. Their uniforms were cobalt blue with the insignia of the triangle and stars above the image of a bird of prey with wings outspread and claws extended.

The chairman, who went by the name of Sibuna, arched his eyebrows as he took command. 'Members of all provinces, stand with your legs apart and place your hands on the desk in front of you. Do not attempt to move until the search is complete.'

He signalled to the soldiers who began searching each of the representatives. Wa-ku could not stand but had placed his belongings on the panel at the front of his hoverchair. A soldier patted him down and inspected the chair as a precaution but found nothing. After a thorough search, the soldiers stepped back to their positions around the chamber and awaited word from Sibuna.

One of the officers moved around the line of soldiers before reporting to the grey-haired chairman who spoke to the man briefly before returning to the microphone.

'Now, I am calling on any witnesses who may have seen or heard anything even mildly suspicious to come forward and tell our senior officer and myself what you have witnessed.'

Wa-ku immediately hovered down the centre aisle to join a small group of other witnesses. They each reported separately until Wa-ku could speak with Sibuna and the senior officer.

'We meet again, Wa-ku,'Sibuna said. 'Now, what was it that you have seen or heard?'

'There was someone in a dark robe behind the pillar there.' Wa-ku pointed out the column where he had seen the assassin emerge.

'I saw him step out with the dart gun ... I tried to warn Maru, but he was too quick. He disappeared somewhere near the back wall; like he just stepped into the floor or something.'

Sibuna nodded. 'Did you get a good look at him?'

Wa-ku shook his head in denial. 'He ... or be it she ... was well cloaked in a dark robe ... hmmm perhaps purple, and I saw no face. It was like a spectre.'

'You say the assassin simply disappeared into the floor?'

'I cannot say for sure ... but one moment he was fleeing, then there was no sign of him.'

Sibuna turned to the senior officer. 'Have your men inspect the floor behind the pillar for any sign of a secret opening. This was not a random thing. Someone knew about what the Ancient was going to say or was afraid of what she might say.'

The officer bowed abruptly and gathered together some of the soldiers who started to inspect the floor closely. One of the men soon found a square seam around a large tile and began attempting to pry it open. Others moved in with tools to remove the tile, but it was stuck fast.

'Stand back!' shouted the senior officer as he withdrew his solar-bite and fired at the tile. The tile erupted into splinters, covering a portion of the floor with debris and revealing a shaft beneath. Several soldiers filed down into the shaft and began to follow it, using their solar-bites as torches. Wa-ku and Sibuna waited nearby until the senior officer returned, frowning.

'The tunnel leads to an abandoned building to the west of the halls, sir,' the officer told Sibuna.

'Our men are searching the area but have found no tracks or anything to lead us to the assassin,' he said.

'Keep looking,' he commanded then turned to Wa-ku. 'Come with me. We will go to the ward and see what Maru's condition is, and if anything has been reported about the dart's origin.'

The senior officer awaited further command as Sibuna prepared to leave. 'What of the provincial representatives, sir? Are they free to leave?'

'Yes, but only to their accommodations. Place two of your men at each door and have them accompany them to any engagements. They must not leave the capital.'

The officer bowed and saluted before informing the soldiers of Sibuna's instructions. Wa-ku and the chairman then left the chamber and continued down the main hall to the outside where they entered a vehicle at a super-conductor station. Wa-ku could mount his chair into the back of the vehicle which was perched over an embedded metal rail in the road pavement. Once activated, the vehicle's super-conductive elements enabled it to float above the rail and travel between stations set within each block. As Kosmo did not comprise massive oceans as on Nerthule, but did possess huge underground water reserves, the sky tended to reflect a mixture of earth tones leaning towards the yellow-blue side of the spectrum. Buildings were made to blend in with the environment and were low-set with vegetation and low bushes sustained on domed roof-lines. Roadways were narrow with parallel rails supporting Conductobiles that could travel to stations set within any part of the city.

Wa-ku and Sibuna alighted at a station in the health quarter, making their way to the medical wards where Maru had been taken. A senior attendant met them and led the way into a room alongside Maru's private ward. Guards had been placed at the door to the ward while crystal digital monitors recorded every movement in and out of the ward. They could see into the room through shatter-proof glass and the bed where Maru lay comatose connected to monitoring equipment.

'How is our honourable Ancient?' Sibuna asked as he peered at the form of the old woman.

'She is stable but until we are able to pinpoint the type of poison, it is impossible to wake her out of her unconscious state. The substance places her in an induced state of suspension as well as complete paralysis.'

'Why did the assassin not simply kill her? I am thankful for her life but what hope is there for her?' Wa-ku said.

Sibuna massaged his chin thoughtfully. 'The traitors, and I say traitors as there must be some group behind this, must want her alive for their own purpose ... but what purpose that is I cannot say. They clearly think she has knowledge they want kept secret.'

'And what of the dart? It would have a trace of the poison, wouldn't it?'Wa-ku asked.

'Yes, but the chemical structure is complex. It will take time to develop an anti-serum.'

A woman in a white robe entered the room, briefly acknowledging Sibuna and Wa-ku before speaking to the attendant.

'We have isolated the chemical agent in the poison,' she said.

'Good, progress ... what have you found?' the attendant asked.

'It is from an insect living in the dark quadrant in the province of Rardarm. A serket wasp. Its sting causes paralysis, allowing it to store the victim for some time before its larvae are hatched and can eat the victim fresh and alive. It would need the toxin from ten wasps to be sufficient to completely paralyse a person.'

'Then the assassin would need access to this wasp toxin from Rardarm ... that's more than a thousand kooniks from here. Not to mention keeping so many of the insects for farming their toxin,' the attendant remarked.

'Yes sir, but that is not all. The insects need to be killed to extract the toxin which is only active for a 20th. They would need to have brought the live insects here to the capital and have extra in case some of the extractions failed or the wasps died in our dry air.'

'Are you saying that the wasps would need to be kept in a special environment to be kept alive?' Sibuna interjected.

'Indeed sir. Humid conditions as in a jungle where it hails.'

Sibuna bent towards Wa-ku. 'Perhaps a plant nursery. I know of several in the capital. I will have the regiment inspect all nurseries, starting with the nearest to the halls. We must find these traitors.'

'And enough serket wasps to develop an anti-serum, sir,' the woman added.

'Yes. Let us hope there are enough wasps to find.'

Wa-ku thought about what his brother had said about the tresoculi rising again. If he had been right about Ra, then there may be a group of tresoculi zealots planning to stage a coup. He decided to ask Sibuna about his suspicions.

'Could this be a group of zealots, sir? Three-eyes working in secret to overthrow us?'

Sibuna gave a considered nod. 'Perhaps your brother colours your opinions, Wa-ku. We have worked together with the tresoculi in peace for hundreds of years. If any are conspiring against us, then they have been cunning in hiding it from the council.'

'If it not be them then someone is conspiring, sir, and succeeding in hiding the fact.'

Sibuna turned briefly to the attendant and the laboratory woman. 'You have done well. I will see to it straight away that we track down these wasps and the traitors.'

He patted Wa-ku on the back. 'Come Wa-ku! We have traitors to catch and wasps to find.'

The pair walked back out and down the hall. 'I do not want to accuse the tresoculi at this time, Wa-ku. We must see what the evidence shows us. There is obviously a disturbed element in the capital.'

* * *

A hot dry wind rustled his golden locks as strands flicked across his face, forcing Wa-ku to brush them away to enable him to witness the drama unfolding before him. He had insisted on accompanying the regiment on their raids but had to wait it out on the street in his hoverchair as the soldiers raided nursery after nursery. This was the fourth nursery they had raided without turning up anything, but this was about to change. The soldiers had been inside for some time, and Wa-ku was looking for a shady spot when he heard the first explosions. Soldiers erupted from the building with solar-bites blazing and received counter-fire from within. Larger solar-flutes emerged from the roofline, shooting magnesium white beams at soldiers who fled for cover as objects disintegrated in front of them. The senior officer yelled at Wa-ku to escape the line of fire. Wa-ku propelled his chair as fast as it could go to a safe distance down the street and behind one of the neighbouring buildings. He felt the ground shake violently. The smell of burning flesh confirmed someone had been hit. He caught sight of a soldier running and crouching, then a blinding beam and smoke. The man was instantly transformed into ashes, and there was a pungent smell of death. 'Now I know why I didn't join the regiment,' he muttered to himself, withdrawing further out of sight. There were further quakes and shouting. Soldiers were retreating en masse, unable to overcome the force of the enemy.

The senior officer glanced at him as he ran past. 'Get the hell out!' he shouted. 'We have to get back-up!' He was waving his arm in a frantic effort to ensure Wa-ku's safety.

Wa-ku felt his heart rushing as he propelled out and away from the scene of destruction. He swivelled around to see what was behind, glimpsing numerous ash heaps that once were men among the debris of pavement where holes had been blasted out of the street. A cloud of dust hung over it all, partially obscuring the nursery. The main vehicle for transporting the soldiers was now a smoking heap of metal. The senior officer clutched a communicator to his ears and mouth as he ran, while Wa-ku swept past him in the hoverchair. Up ahead he could see a conductobile which would lead him away from danger. Black robed zealots stepped out onto the street behind them and raised their fists in triumph. Wa-ku felt the heat of a nearby soldier been struck, then a flash of dust. He tasted the acid from his stomach as it rose into his throat. His heart was pumping as he docked with the conductible and tapped in the address of military headquarters, his fingers trembling. *I don't wish to die today.* He input the fastest speed.

The conductobile whirred into motion then shuddered. Wa-ku was blinded as a fire rose around him. Metal melted. The street swirled around in a blur. He clutched his chair, but he could not withstand the inertia of being flung sideways and around. There were a few moments of suspension before the mass of machinery hit the ground, grinding into pavement while Wa-ku slipped free and smashed into the unforgiving earth. Metal fragments gouged into his shoulder and sliced his face open. Wa-ku cried out as sharp pain impacted him. He felt the wetness on his cheek before the world withdrew into unconsciousness. When he woke up, there were men carrying him on a stretcher and loading him into the back of a vehicle. He saw Sibuna leaning over him, frowning. 'You satisfied now? Nearly got yourself killed, you fool.'

Wa-ku found himself in the wards when he gained consciousness again. His face was numb from anaesthetic and covered in a healing gel while gauze was wrapped around his injured shoulder. He winced as he tried to turn his head to see towards the door where two military guards were posted. A nurse was fussing about taking his vitals while noting heart rate on a nearby monitor. When she noticed his eyes flicker open, she smiled, revealing dimples under large brown ovals.

'Good to see you awake, Wa-ku!' she chirped. 'Is it true you have been to Mareos and Thenigmas?'

Wa-ku groaned in his lethargy. 'I have travelled, yes,' he mumbled.

'Oh, how I would love to be there. Is Mareos beautiful?'

'In a manner of speaking, I suppose it is. There are vast forests ... and even the wasteland is littered with gemstones and crystal.'

Her brown eyes widened. 'Oh, what a delight!'

Wa-ku's face felt taut as he grinned. She was like a breath of fresh air.

'Perhaps I can show you sometime,' he ventured, and was immediately rewarded with her beaming smile. Her lips parted, showing a perfect set of bleached teeth, and her straight black hair was tied up into her bonnet.

'I'd like that. I will remind you when you are better.'

Wa-ku's eyes followed the curve of her slim body as she turned and left the room, passing Sibuna as he marched in towards him.

'I see you have decided to rejoin the living,' the grey-haired elder remarked.

'Something like that,' Wa-ku muttered.

'It was touch and go, my friend. I should never have let you accompany the raids, but then we never expected what happened.' Sibuna sat down on a chair alongside the bed.

'We have to get you a new chair. It was totally wrecked, and we lost ten good men in the raid. And there's more bad news since you have been lying here having a good time.'

'Hardly a good time ... anyway I was out to it all,' Wa-ku retorted.

'Yes, as I said ... while you were lying here for days, things have gotten worse. The Black Brotherhood, as they call themselves, have been attacking our facilities ... guerrilla style. We've had to shut down the city and put out a curfew. No-one is allowed on the street unless accompanied by our soldiers.'

Wa-ku huffed. 'What! I can't believe it ...'

'Oh, it's true all right,' the elder assured. 'And what's more, Yidu has escaped. We believe the brotherhood aided in his escape, and he is plotting against the state.'

'He escaped? How? The fortifications!' Wa-ku shook his head, and immediately regretted it as he fell back in pain.

Sibuna's features were grim. 'Destroyed. The brotherhood blasted their way in and killed all the border guards.'

Wa-ku sighed. 'It is just as Maru foretells. We are doomed.'

'The Black Brotherhood has amassed superior weaponry right under our noses. We are at war, but we will ... we must ... conquer them.'

The man in the bed sneered. 'The tresoculi. Yidu is behind this.'

Sibuna hesitated. 'It is only an element. We cannot say that they are all tresoculi.'

'Not tresoculi! Wake up old man! They have been planning this for a long time.'

The elder looked away. 'We must not anger those in the council. I could never accuse them of betrayal. The duoculi have had no issue with them. They are beyond reproach.'

'I would not trust any of them now. You should keep them out of any discussions. Keep only the duoculi informed.'

Sibuna was dismissive. 'That would drive them towards the enemy. We cannot risk such a thing.'

Wa-ku's eyes glowed with ire. 'The enemy is already lying in our beds and eating at our tables!'

The elder surveyed his colleague with compassion. 'I can understand your feelings, Wa-ku. We must test everyone for their loyalty. No-one, including the duoculi, can be fully trusted. These are dire times.'

The nurse returned to check the monitor, forcing Wa-ku to tone down as he admired her cheerful nature.

'Perhaps you are right honoured one,' Wa-ku conceded. 'Diplomacy is best, but we need to keep on our toes.'

The nurse stole glances at them as she went about her duties, singing softly to herself.

Sibuna's mouth wrinkled up in a half smile as he noticed the change in Wa-ku's attitude. 'Such creatures as angels do soothe the savage nature,' he said, winking at him.

Wa-ku did not answer but felt a little flushed at the thought of he and the young nurse.

Their conversation was abruptly cut short by loud shouting in the hallways.

'The Black Brotherhood has come to cut out the tongue of the ancient one!' a male voice cried, and a chorus of others answered it. 'Hail Ra!'

Sibuna stood up. 'Take cover nurse!' he commanded the young woman as her eyes expressed alarm.

The elder took a sheet and covered Wa-ku with it. 'You are too easy a target. Better they think you dead already,' he said, as he ducked behind the bed, gesturing to the nurse, who still stood frozen, to join him.

'Oh dear,' she squeaked. 'What is happening!'

When Sibuna realised her fear, he pulled her over to him and forced her to duck behind Wa-ku's bed. The sheet he had used to cover Wa-ku also fell to the floor on one side, concealing them from view.

There were more shouts, crashing of glass and equipment as the men made their way up the nearby hallway. 'Where is Maru?' they heard one of them ask another. 'Down the next hallway, there,' the other answered.

'Halt!' a guard said.

The building rocked, and the room lit up for a moment as a solar-bite blast did its damage. Then in the next seconds a melee broke out, turning the hospice into a war zone. Blasts came in waves, shattering glass panels in the ward and showering them with particles from the ceiling. The nurse hugged the elder in fright, trembling and sobbing. Sibuna patted her like a child, trying to keep her calm.

'You're safe here, child. They are not after you. Just keep quiet.'

She nodded with her head buried into his chest. 'I'll try,' she whispered.

The shooting had stopped but it was clear that all the guards had been overcome as the jumble of victorious cries came from the brotherhood members.

'Oh no,' Sibuna said. 'They've got her.'

'Careful,' a voice spoke. 'Get her to the back exit quick. We can't risk the front way ... it'll be crawling with the military soon.'

The voices gradually diminished down another hallway leading to the back, replaced by the thunder of soldiers' feet from the front. Sibuna sighed, rose to his feet and pulled the sheet back off Wa-ku, only to meet a man's haunted stare. The nurse was still clutching on to the elder. She had waited this long, but now let go with a gush of tears and moans.

'It's okay dear. They've left now. You're safe.'

Sibuna gently pushed her away, leaving her to collapse in a sobbing heap on the nearest chair.

Wa-ku felt her pain but was unable to reach out to comfort her. He glanced back at Sibuna and rolled his eyes, shocked.

'Now they have Maru. What are they to do with her?' His question was more rhetorical as he knew that Sibuna was as clueless as he was as to the answer.

A group of soldiers ran past the ward to witness the scene of devastation ahead. A senior officer returned and entered the ward. He bowed to Sibuna. 'We are too late. What has happened here, sir?'

'The brotherhood has taken Maru. Do you have any more news of incursions?'

'We were able to capture one of the zealots, sir, but he poisoned himself before we could question him.'

'And what of his identity? Was he ...?'

'Tresoculi sir.'

The officer confirmed Sibuna's fear.

Sibuna rubbed his forehead. 'What do these people want? I do not understand.'

'It must have something to do with Ra's grab for power. They are diverting our attention and costing us precious time,' Wa-ku replied.

The nurse lifted her head, revealing a face awash with tears. 'Ra? Is he not dead these thousands of years?'

'He has risen from a cosmic sleep and wants absolute power over the planetary triad,' Wa-ku said.

'That's terrible,' she said, not fully comprehending what it all meant.

Sibuna put a soft hand on her shoulder. 'You best clean yourself up, my dear. The patient will be all right for now.'

She stood, bowed to the elder chairman and quickly exited the ward. Sibuna raised weary eyes to the senior officer.

'Gather the cosmo-ship fleet commanders and meet me at the Halls of Ra at two-twentieths from now. Wa-ku is right. We cannot delay any longer. I am declaring a global emergency.'

The officer bowed and left, leaving only the two men in the ward. Wa-ku struggled to pull himself up to a sitting position. 'How long before I have a new chair? I must get on my ship and go to Nerthule for Mirrortac. We must put a stop to all this.'

'You can't go anywhere for a while, I'm afraid. We will arrange someone to take care of your furred friends.'

'I must go. I owe it to them. Just carry me to the ship. I can operate the controls from a static seat.'

Sibuna saw Wa-ku's imploring eyes. 'I wish I could. You are still recovering from serious wounds. It would be impossible, I'm afraid.'

Wa-ku felt dejected. 'If only I had not gone on those stupid raids,' he muttered.

Sibuna could only nod his agreement. 'You are right there,' he said. 'Get some rest. Enjoy your recuperation. You have a beautiful young woman taking care of you.'

Wa-ku took no joy from this. All he could think of now was what Ra and his brother Yidu had planned.

* * *

The main chamber was filled with commanders of the cosmo-ship fleet plus the highest-ranking officers of the Uranian order of the Universal Guardians. They were all robed in white tied at the waist with long red sashes. Sibuna himself had swapped his brown robe of justice to the white robe, and now wore a crown of black jade with two prominences like pointed ears. By declaring a global emergency, he now assumed the position of supreme commander of all Uranian forces.

His blue eyes had paled as he surveyed the gathering from the centre podium.

'Force commanders of Kosmo and the Uranian order of the Universal Guardians, we are here on a matter most urgent. Zealots have thwarted the open council's deliberation to rescue the triad from the machinations of a resurrected Ra. I have declared this global emergency to expedite this action without further recourse to the full council of the provinces. I am issuing this command that all in charge of cosmo-ship forces fully arm their craft for dispatch to Nerthule, effective immediately.'

A gabble of voices rose in the chamber as commanders and officers discussed this latest development. A lower ranked officer entered the chamber, bowed to Sibuna, then strode quickly to one of the commanders, giving him an official note. The commander read it and immediately approached the supreme commander. The man bowed. 'Sir, we have received grave news that many of our ships have been sabotaged, and a fleet of unknown craft have been seen leaving Kosmo for points unknown.'

Sibuna frowned. 'Are there any ships left operable commander?'

'Only some that were undergoing maintenance, sir.'

'Did anyone see how many of the unknown craft there were?'

'Observers say several hundred, sir.'

Sibuna slammed his fists down on the podium and swore. 'Where do these ships come from? We must have intel on these zealots. Surely someone knows something!'

The commander appeared awkward but stood tall. 'All we know is that they appear to come from the far province of Sek in the Ovodian Wastelands.'

The elder was thoughtful. 'That province is 90 per cent tresoculi. Why have we not suspected this ...' he muttered, more to himself than the commander.

Sibuna slowly raised his eyes to the assemblage and scanned the faces of the commanders. After running his eyes over the crowd several times, he turned back to the commander before him.

'Where are the tresoculi fleet commanders? There are none here.'

The commander looked from side to side, bemused. 'Er, all commanders were informed, sir.'

Sibuna steepled his fingers, pressing them against his lips in thought. 'I did not want to believe our three-eyed brothers and sisters would slip into old ways. But all along they have been conspiring against us, waiting for Ra and Yidu to signal the beginning of their traitorous actions.'

The elder grabbed the microphone to address the crowd. 'Good duoculi commanders, we have been cunningly deceived. Our ships have been compromised; sabotaged. We must work in haste to restore them as the tresoculi have gone on before us ... they have built their own fleet and are now headed for Nerthule. All remaining tresoculi and their sympathisers are to be arrested and held until this mess is cleaned up.'

* * *

The nurse crept into the ward, trying to avoid eye contact with Wa-ku as he sat trying to eat some breakfast. With eyes downcast she approached his bedside to examine his wounds.

'I am sorry, sir, that I was so emotional yesterday. You have enough concern than for a nurse to be so unprofessional.'

Wa-ku moved his hand under her chin and lifted it up so that she would look at him. 'You have nothing to be sorry for, miss. An attack such as you witnessed would terrify anyone.'

The woman's lips trembled with a hint of a smile. 'You are most kind.'

Wa-ku smiled, withdrawing his hand. 'And what be your name, miss?'

'Hathor,' she ventured shyly.

'Well Hathor, I am glad that I am in such good hands.'

She giggled while inspecting the wound on his face. 'It is healing well. You will soon be walking around.'

Wa-ku pulled back his bed sheet, showing useless legs. 'Not with these, Hathor. That was thanks to an accident a long time ago.'

Hathor threw her hands over her mouth as she gasped. 'Oh, sorry. I did not mean ...'

'It's okay. Once I get my new chair I will be out and about again.'

A computer nearby activated, beeping as data spread out across the screen. Hathor was distracted and looked over to the screen with annoyance.

'Excuse me, I must attend to this. It should not be doing that,' she said.

She walked over to the screen and stared at it, biting her lip and muttering to herself. 'What is this! Someone must be playing a joke.'

Wa-ku arched his head over to spy Hathor's frowning face. 'What is the problem?'

She scratched her head. 'It is text, but there are symbols. I do not understand what it's saying.'

The screen continued to fill up with the strange text before remotely activating a printer which zipped into action, shuffling and spilling out pages of the text.

'Here, hand over those pages,' Wa-ku directed.

Hathor did as he asked, placing the pages in front of the man. Wa-ku perused the text, noting the symbols and text were from an ancient dialect that was reminiscent of what he had seen on the Three Stones of Destiny.

'Can you call the museum ... and the supreme commander. We need an interpreter of ancient texts, and the commander needs to see this.'

* * *

The curator was a short woman with grey-green eyes and thin lips. Wa-ku and Sibuna looked on as she pored over the pages, examining the text carefully.

'Hmmm, most interesting,' she said, taking out a magnifier to scrutinise the symbols.

'It is from the Ancients. You say this came over the display. Who has access to the system?' Large eyes rested on Hathor who was standing nearby.

'Oh, only the clinical staff, ma'am. And no-one learns old dialects.'

'Hmmm, most interesting,' the old woman repeated.

'Well, spill it out. Do you know what it says?' Sibuna was getting impatient.

The curator raised a thin arm. 'Calm down your honour. What is it that the Nerthulians said ... er, "Rome was not built in a day".'

'Do you understand any of it?' he pushed.

The woman nodded. 'Yes, I do. This appears to be a message from an Ancient still living. It speaks of sacred stones and the need to destroy them, as a great heresy has been committed. The symbols represent the triad and the three stones. It warns that this ancient one is about to be awakened and forced to look upon the Pool of Knowledge to gauge the movements of the Universal Guardians and thwart all attempts to stop them.'

Wa-ku and Sibuna regarded each other with expressions of horror. 'That is why they have kept Maru alive ... to look into the future and cut off all possibilities of a duoculi victory,' Sibuna said.

'Oh, there is another symbol here ...' the old woman interjected.

All eyes returned to the curator.

'It is the sword and the Veil, meaning a violent sacrifice that will take someone beyond death. I believe the Ancient intends to end her life to save the triad.'

FAKERY REVEALED

The erfins had learned much about Nerthule and its inhabitants since their rapid departure from Egypt and their arrival in an isolated part of the US. Mirrortac knew that although one could travel at amazing speed from place to place, the wheels of officialdom were more maddening than the incessant prattle of the Petros people on his home planet, where introductions meant telling your life story. He learned that the world was divided into portions that belonged to each group of people, and no-one from one portion could travel to another without permission, which meant waiting many moons for a parchment inscribed with each permission and including the magical likeness of that person. Raul had agreed to bringing the stone to the US and allowing Mirrortac to examine it and describe its purpose, but again permissions had to be sought, and special security measures taken. Raul would accompany the stone and communicate his own findings to US researchers.

The people at the US facility were taking good care of Mirrortac and his family. They no longer slept in a shielded room, but one with soft bedding for each of them, and sweet-scented liquids for them to douse on their bodies in what the humans insisted be a daily bathing ritual. None of them minded, particularly Treetam, who loved to sniff the various perfumes and dab her face as the human women did. Her brothers found this amusing, and liked to make fun of her strange colourings, but Ameece rebuked them as she thought the pastel hues enhanced Treetam's features in an alluring fashion. Sometimes a human would intervene to advise about the quantity of what they called 'make-up', as Treetam would often dab on copious amounts around her eyes and on her cheeks. The make-up did not go as well on fur as it did on a woman's bare face, but when used sparingly, the effect could be described as positive.

Food preparation was at first problematic, as the Nerthulians' proclivity for cooking everything made it unpalatable for them, and when they were served raw produce and meat, it also made them ill. The humans at last resorted to what they described as 'organic' foods, and this was successful. However, none of the Nerthulians would sit at table with them when they ate, preferring not to be present for reasons that bewildered Mirrortac and his family.

Healers would come each day to test and prod each of them and test their alien microbes for any threats to the populace of Nerthule. The quarantine was maintained, which meant that they could venture freely within the compound, but not anywhere externally.

* * *

Raul Haru arrived in the pre-dawn, accompanied by two Egyptian security officers and the Australian astrobiologist James Kelly. One of the officers carried a metal box that had been secured to his wrist with handcuffs. They were shown into the main operations room where Mirrortac and his kin had originally met with the American contingent. They had already been made to wear protective masks and sat at table with Danielle King and an American agent. Mirrortac was the only one of his family asked to sit with them. He arched bushy eyebrows at the sight of the box and guessed at its contents.

'You have brought the Einuk stone?' He met the enigmatic dark eyes of the Egyptian curator.

Raul inclined his head in a slight bow to the erfin. 'That I have. And you are this creature who claims possession of the stone?' he asked back.

Kelly grinned at the erfin. 'Good to see ya again, mate. I hope they are taking good care of you here,' he winked.

Mirrortac bowed at the Australian, then noticed there was something glistening on the man's neck. He stared at it for a few moments, endeavouring to fathom out what it was before realising it was some gemstone-type adornment. He then turned his attention and mind towards the curator, tuning in as best he could to the man's thoughts to determine his nature. Raul appeared to be aware of Mirrortac's attempts to enter his thoughts, momentarily scrutinising the erfin with a dark suspicious stare before showing a hint of a smile. The erfin felt a stabbing pain in his head as his attempts at mind reading failed.

'You are a most interesting fellow,' Raul said as he gave a contained smile.

'And what is this interest you have in this stone?'

Mirrortac decided to be cagey as there was something about Raul that was not quite right. 'It was taken from us and must be returned. It is part of a set of sacred stones which must be kept together,' he explained, watching the curator's face closely as he said this.

Raul's eyes flared for a moment before he leaned across the table towards the erfin. 'I have dated this stone, and it has been within its sarcophagus under the sea here for thousands of years. Are you saying that you are thousands of years old? How do I know that you speak the truth?'

'Yea ... it went missing from our world beyond the count of many moons. Why would I naught speak the truth?' Mirrortac countered.

'Is it not true that it was put here as a device to provide fast travel between far distant planets? Is this not what you told my distinguished colleague here.' Raul gestured with his hand to indicate Kelly seated beside him. 'Indeed, is it not your method of travelling here from your planet?'

Mirrortac shrugged. 'It has led us here to your world, yes. But now we wish to take it home.'

Raul mocked him with a laugh. 'And how do you propose to do this, erfin? If it is your means of travel, then you cannot simply take it with you.'

The erfin sighed, looking down at the table. 'You speak truth. We must wait upon others to come to our aid. Perhaps *you* can help us?'

Raul laughed again. 'I am a mere student of past cultures in this planet of ours, but even our greatest advances in science would take you years just to reach the outer reaches of our solar system let alone the vast distances to other stars.'

The erfin was a little bemused at Raul's comment. 'Then we wait ...'

The smile left Raul's face. Was it a flash of gold light that Mirrortac saw behind the turban, or simply the glint off his turban gemstone? The erfin felt suddenly uneasy. This was the first Nerthulian whose mind was blocked to him.

Raul looked up at the security guard with the metal box containing the stone.

'Perhaps it is time for us to show you the stone that has brought us all together here today. We can then discuss it further.'

He nodded at the guard who moved forward and placed the box on the table. Raul produced a key and unlocked the cuffs before keying in a code on a device attached to the box. The locks on the box released, allowing him to open it up. All present watched as an orange-hued stone was revealed, presenting its characteristic swirled icon and smooth curved sides. Mirrortac frowned at the crude design and abruptly stood up.

'This stone is untrue! Where is the true one?' he growled, startling the others.

King narrowed her eyes at the curator. 'What? Is this a fake?'

Raul looked around casually. 'I would prefer to say this is an accurate replica. We could not chance moving such a valuable piece of antiquity from Egypt.'

King blushed red. 'You were ordered to bring the real stone here. I believe Mirrortac has established just this moment that he has intimate knowledge of the Einuk stone.'

Raul was unmoved. 'This antiquity belongs to Egypt. I am sorry, but our authorities would not release it.'

'Then this whole ruse with the cuffs and the key-coded case was designed to fool us into thinking we had the real stone. Such arrogance!' King huffed.

'Oh, it was no ruse, Miss King. This replica shows in reasonably accurate detail what the original appears like, and therefore its design is still "classified information" as you Americans would say ... so we had to take precautions.'

'What a load of bull!' King roared. 'You are deliberately hampering the United Nations. I can bring you up before the international court, Mr Haru.'

Raul put up his hands to appease her. 'Now, now, Miss King. You will do no such thing. You Americans think that you can interfere with our national rights and bully us smaller nations. I will offer you a peace pipe ... here.' He opened another compartment in the case and produced several rings bearing exquisite gemstones.

King was suspicious. 'What is this? Some token ... Are you bribing us?'

The curator presented his most charming smile. 'I would not do that, Miss King. I simply wish to offer these as gifts to you and your staff. And invite you and the erfin here to visit the real stone at the Cairo museum and stay in our best accommodations as a guest of Egypt.'

Her hazel eyes drifted to the shining rings. 'Sorry Mr Haru. We cannot accept gifts from international representatives, but we may take you up on a visit to see the real stone as a compromise.'

The Egyptian bowed. 'I understand. But at least try it on for size. I know you will like it. And then you can give it back if you wish.' He picked out a ring and offered it to her.

King hesitated before accepting the ring in her hand. 'Okay ... just to see how it looks, mind you. Then you get it back.'

Raul inclined his head again in a bow. 'Certainly.'

Mirrortac felt his chest tighten as King toyed with the ring before placing it on her finger. She gasped for a moment as though hit with a shock before her expression changed, and she nodded, smiling at Raul.

'You are right master. You are most generous. Thank you for this great gift.'

Mirrortac's silvan eyebrows raised quizzically. '*Master?*' he thought. '*Why would she address him as though she be a servant?*'

King turned to Mirrortac. 'We have misjudged our visitor. Shall we accompany him back to Egypt?'

'If the true Einuk stone is there, then I and my kin will follow,' he said, now feeling an almost overwhelming sense of foreboding.

Raul took a more masculine sculpted ring and offered it to the agent alongside King. He looked to her strangely before being drawn to accept the ring. Again, there was a subtle jolt in his body when he put on the ring, with the same change in demeanour. Mirrortac saw the Egyptian withdraw a much larger ring that clearly would fit his stubby finger, but as Raul started to present the ring towards him, he began dismissing it and backed away from the table.

'You must grant me leave, as I am feeling quite illsome just now,' Mirrortac explained as he started to turn and walk away.

He caught Raul pouting in annoyance before ignoring his outstretched hand. The erfin's mind was racing with panic, and it took all his resolve to stay calm and walk away. He was afraid of what sorcery was enmeshed in the rings that immediately predisposed anyone who wore a ring to serve the Egyptian. He could hear King calling after him. 'What's the matter?' she was saying. 'Come back ... get your ring'. And now she was calling other staff to wear rings. Mirrortac knew Raul was using the rings to mesmerise all those who up to now had worked with him to gain the Einuk stone.

The erfin picked up his pace as he approached the family bed chamber where the others awaited him. He pounded his fists together in agitation as the realisation dawned on him that Raul was no ordinary Nerthulian. Those eyes. The arrogant posture. He'd seen it before. Raul ... RA–ul!

Ameece looked up as Mirrortac entered the chamber. She saw that he was agitated and walked up to comfort him. 'What has happened? Did you see the stone?'she said.

Mirrortac shook his head and slumped onto the bed, causing it to creak loudly. 'Ra is here. He pretends to be a man from the hall of ancient things. He has Einuk but brought a useless rock here!'

Ameece peered at her he-erfin with incredulity. The triplets also gathered around after hearing the news.

'Then we tell Danielle he is Ra,' she said.

But Mirrortac's bloodshot eyes betrayed despair. 'He brought small stones enmeshed with sorcery. He has all here under his power. They will serve Ra now.'

'Then our place here is in danger. We must find a way out of here,' Mitac advised.

Ezof cheered at the thought of escape. 'Let us take their weapons and battle our way out of here!'

'And how will we do that, bro?' Mitac cautioned.

'Um ... you think of a way,' Ezof said.

Treetam sighed. 'I do not wish to kill any more of these men. I still have bad dreams of what happened at Thenigmas.'

'No-one is killing anyone,' Ameece said. 'These Nerthulians are good, but if they are under Ra's command, then ... then ... I do not know.'

Mirrortac buried his face into his big hands. 'It be hopeless,' he muttered. 'Einuk is now beyond our reach. We can naught fight Ra.'

Mitac paced around the room with his head down. 'I don't believe that our place here is for nothing. There must be a way.'

A shout went up from another part of the compound followed by the sound of footfall that echoed up the hall until it was clear that several Nerthulians were making for the erfins'chamber. Mirrortac raised his head towards the doorway where he could see guards armed with guns making a grim march into the room.

'Get up!' one of them yelled, pointing his gun directly at Mirrortac. 'All of you!' he added, and the other guards also cocked their guns at them.

The erfins stood nonplussed to regard the guards. The men rounded them up and roughly directed them out of the room and down the hall to another room where the bedding was more spartan and the walls a drab grey.

'This is your new quarters from now on,' the head guard growled. 'Miss King will be with you shortly.'

'It has begun,' Mirrortac whispered.

Two guards stood at the door, regarding the erfins with condescension. They swayed their guns towards them with menace. 'No trying anything, aliens. These will kill you instantly,' one man warned.

The erfins all stood frozen to the spot while the guards continued to harass them. King soon appeared between them, her face a grim mask in stark contrast to her former friendly poise.

'We heard what you have planned for us. You are plotting to kill us and escape this facility. Raul has filled me in on your plan to steal the Einuk stone and destabilise the world. You are now officially a threat to international security and will be kept imprisoned here until we can work out what to do with you.'

Mirrortac pulled at the white fur on his head. 'You be mistaken she-one. Raul wants the stone himself to turn you all into slaves. He is ruling your minds with those gems of his ...'

King shook her head in denial, sending dark curls flying about her head. 'No! No! I will hear none of your lies, erfins! Goodnight!' At that she turned heel and marched back down the hall. The guards shut the door on them and locked it with a resounding clunk.

Mitac's forehead furrowed. 'How can these Nerthulians hear what we say in our bed chamber? Do the walls have ears?'

'T'would seem so,' Mirrortac mused before swinging around and clutching Mitac.

'*Stop talking! We speak and listen with our minds from this time,*' he said, using telepathy.

Mitac's eyes went wide. '*Ah papa. This will be our way out of this. They use magic devices to listen to us; let them tune to our minds!*'

'*That is good son. But remember to keep it between us ... Ra can listen too.*'

'*Were we not speaking erfinish?*' Ameece quiried.

'*Ra must be able, like us, to discern all tongues.*'

ESCAPE IN NERTHULE

zof struggled to open the door of their cell but to no avail. It had been many days since their internment. Guards shoved a tray of meat under the door each day, while the bathing ritual had been reduced to unceremoniously dousing them with water sprayed at them with a sinuous pipe that looked more like a snake with a metal mouth. Ameece had again tried to use the communication stone to contact the roznoghs but to no avail. It clearly needed the proximity of the Einuk stone to allow any contact.

The erfins and Ameece were moping around the cell when they heard footsteps approaching down the hall. Treetam edged into a corner of the cell, trembling. '*I do not wish to be watered like some plant,*' she said.

Everyone stiffened as the door lock clunked open, and they waited for the inevitable flood of water.

'Come quickly guys. We're getting out of here,' a voice said.

They looked up to see the grinning face of the Australian astrobiologist. His face broke into wrinkles that spread out from his eyes and mouth.

Mirrortac hesitated as he scanned the friendly face. 'What is happening? Has Ra summoned us?' The erfin frowned.

'Bugger Ra. We have work to do and too little time to do it. Now, come on.' Kelly motioned to them to leave the cell and follow him down the hall.

They all made a timid exit, exchanging confused glances as they went out into the hall. Kelly continued to urge them forward while they all advanced nervously, expecting to be stopped at any time.

The Australian winked at them with a broad grin. 'Don't worry cobbers. No-one is going to come at you. Trust me.'

Ameece clutched Mirrortac closely as they made their way down the hall and past the conference area. The triplets came in close behind, eyeing a guard as they neared him. The guard simply watched, with his weapon at ease by his side. They passed more guards who were likewise disinterested until they bypassed the quarantine station and came upon an open area where a black vehicle was parked. Kelly opened the doors to the vehicle and motioned for them to enter. He smiled as he took the front driver's seat and pressed a device to open the large gateway. The vehicle moved away and through the gateway into the night. The tinted windows blocked much of the view outside, but again Kelly pressed a button, which withdrew the transparent shades into the doors, letting in a rush of cool air and an open view of hills and vegetation.

Mirrortac looked up astounded. 'You do not fear disease as you call it?'

Kelly's eyes smiled from the rear vision mirror. 'The danger has passed. You deserve to breathe and smell the earth's rich scents and air,' he said.

The erfin sensed a change that was not due to Ra's influence.

'How can it be that you defy Ra when his stone is clasped to you?'

'You'll get your answers soon enough my friends. For now, just enjoy the drive.'

Silhouettes of trees and hills blurred past, and along with it drifted the heavy scent of exotic plants and the lingering ammonia odour of animal dung. Mirrortac and his kin sucked in the various smells that were both familiar and alien. In the indigo sky, they saw unfamiliar patterns of stars, including a stream of numerous stars that curved above them like some celestial necklace.

The gentle movement of the vehicle and the soothing visions of the night lulled the furred kin into dreams that took them into the dawn. Soon they were rubbing sleepy eyes as their Australian driver came to a stop. Their surrounds were shrouded in a thick fog as a shining gold disc made feeble penetration into the new morning.

'Time to stretch your legs, fellas. Then I'll attend to rustling up some grub for breakfast,' Kelly said, alighting from the car and opening the passenger doors.

'You will feed us grubs?' Mitac quizzed, squinting up under droopy eyelids.

Kelly laughed. 'Not grubs literally, my little mates. But something I'm sure you'll like.'

'I could eat a whole fote,' Ezof said as he stumbled out onto the ground.

Treetam bent down and dug her fingers into the soft earth, sniffing it.

'Oh, it is so pleasing to feel the earth again.'

Ameece stared around her at the small shrubs nearby. 'It is, my sweet. And none of the White Veil, except this mistness.'

Mirrortac's paw-hand supported his hip as he limped off after Kelly who led the way through the shrubs and towards a dark shape ahead of them.

'You are a strange Nerthulian, James Kelly. I hope this tale of how you have avoided Ra's sorcery is a convincing one. Or be it that you possess stronger sorcery?'

Kelly glanced behind and smiled but did not answer. He led on until the dark shape took the form of a wood cabin. The fragrance of fir was unmistakable and transported the elder erfin back to his days in Eol where the conifers grew thickly in the surrounding woodland. He thought of his two daughters left behind, and now back in Eol after returning from the Faug Forest. Ameece supported her erfin as he struggled in the chill air. The triplets whispered to each other as they discussed the vegetation and their first experience of being in the wilds of this alien planet.

The Australian opened the cabin door and indicated for them to enter.

'You guys make yourself comfortable inside while I get you something to eat ... well, I am hoping that it will be something if it worked,' he corrected.

The triplets hustled inside before Ameece and Mirrortac lumbered in. The spartan interior comprised a single large room with a fireplace, bed, food preparation area and some basic crafted timber seating. Although the fireplace was not blazing, there were still red embers simmering amid the ashes, and wood stacked up nearby for a new fire. Ameece took some of the wood and loaded it carefully upon the embers, blowing softly with her breath to set the embers glowing and sputtering. The smaller sticks near the embers gradually came alight, new flames licking around them until it was hot enough for the larger pieces to burn. Soon the fire had taken hold, spreading light and warmth into the cabin.

Mirrortac moved closer to the fire, rubbing his aching bones as the soothing heat soaked into his legs and arms.

'Your mind recalls Yenic's skill with the hearth,' he said.

Ameece turned to him and nuzzled him with a smile. 'I have no true memory of this, yet I know it.'

The door burst open to reveal Kelly armed with small animal carcasses strung up and hanging from a metal rod.

'The traps worked. We will all eat well this morning,' he huffed. 'Ah, I see you have got a fire going already. Most impressive!' he grinned.

Ezof grinned widely at the dead offering. 'And this also is most impressive, as you say, James Kelly.'

Kelly had barely extracted the carcasses when he was crowded by eager hands snatching up the meaty morsels. He left them to claw and rip at the food as he approached the fire with his own.

'If you don't mind, I'd rather cook mine. It's a human thing, you understand.' He pushed his breakfast into the embers fur and all.

'What name do you give this creature?' Mirrortac asked, gnawing off its head.

Kelly looked back then abruptly away. 'We call them rabbits. It is okay to kill them because they are in large numbers as they breed quickly.'

Ezof raised an eyebrow. 'Is it not "okay" to eat some animals?'

'Some animals are few in number, and we do not kill them because it is important for them to keep the balance in nature.'

'Curious,' Mitac mused. 'That humans would care so much for creatures but kill each other.'

Kelly smiled. 'You have great wisdom my little furry friend.'

'I can speak with the creatures,' Mirrortac muttered, still enjoying the rabbit flesh.

The others stared at the elder erfin, but Kelly simply smiled to himself.

'Oh yes,' Mirrortac went on matter-of-factly. 'I spoke with the spirit of a Wooil once. The creature was killing the roznoghs and I pleaded with the spirit to stop; it would not ... but it gave me the secret to killing it, so the spirit could go to another to make up the "balance".'

The triplets all shook their heads, nonplussed. 'Dada, you are wonderous! What be this Wooil of which you speak?' Treetam said.

'It is a big fat creature with sharp teeth and clawed paws as big as your head,' Mirrortac replied, widening his arms to communicate the great size of the bovine beast.

Ameece patted the elder erfin's shoulder with affection. 'I know the Wooil, as it lives in the land of my people, the roznoghs. It is indeed fiercesome, and I too am filled with wonder that this hero of mine was able to kill it.'

'And you talked to its spirit?' Kelly injected.

The erfin nodded.

'You are indeed no ordinary erfin, my friend.' Kelly seemed thoughtful, absently poking at the rabbit sizzling in the fire.

'And you be no normal Nerthulian,' Mirrortac half smiled. 'You are about to tell us how you can defy Ra with that stone on your neck when even one who calls herself adviser to the leader of this America falls under his sorcery.'

Kelly inclined his head at the erfin and gave a salute. 'And this I will reveal, although nobody in this world other than you and a few special exceptions will know it. You see, this crystal here,' he said, fingering the stone on his neck, 'has no effect on the ancestors of ones such as Ra, since we are the ones who devised all power crystals in the first place.'

Mirrortac sat up straight, raising his eyebrows. 'You are ...'

'An Ancient ... yes. But this body was born in this world, and I'm afraid I babble like an Aussie because that is my natural upbringing.'

The elder erfin stroked his snowy beard in thought. 'I am told of these ones ... the Ancients ... and the Three Stones of Destiny ... you made them?'

'We ... we made them, yes,' Kelly corrected. 'My spirit inhabits this body, but I have dwelt in many bodies, and many on this Earth, or Nerthule as we properly proclaim this sphere. I originally came here as guardian of Einuk, to ensure that the stone is properly protected and not misused. I knew of Ra and his great nephew Yidu and their plans but could not intervene as Ra had found Einuk and put it in his resurrection sarcophagus with him.'

Mirrortac blinked and clutched his head. 'I thought the Ancients to be wise spirits, but all dead to the body.'

Kelly steepled his fingers in front of his solemn face. 'Most of us live only in the spirit realm, but some choose to dwell again in human bodies to act directly such as in my case. Unfortunately, I have to keep renewing bodies here as the Nerthulian barely attains a hundred Earth years, unlike my Uranian heritage which ensures thousands of years.'

The triplets were open-mouthed at Kelly's revelation, but Ameece listened attentively.

'We too have nine lives, James Kelly,' she said. 'It is the power of you Ancients that shows us our former lives through the Werdstone.'

Kelly nodded. 'Indeed, Ameece. The knowledge of my sisters abides in the Werdstone, but this knowledge was never meant for mere roznoghs or erfins to possess. Yidu contaminated our stone of power to mesmerise and control you as Ra seeks to do to the people of this world. You see, the knowledge and power in the Werdstone and the Three Stones of Destiny are stored there to protect, but if harnessed and released, are so absolute that nobody except an Ancient can withstand it.'

'Yes, I felt the power in the Werdstone. It makes me shiver to think of it now.' Mirrortac shook his head.

Ameece gave an accusing glance at her erfin. 'Did make me shiver too! I feared what it did to you.'

Kelly nodded sagely. 'Its power is indeed intoxicating, my friend. You are lucky you had it for only a short time.'

Mirrortac frowned. 'Yet Ameece was not affected.'

Kelly waved a hand in dismissal. 'She was affected, but Yidu controlled it. He exercised his power through all the "daughters of the Werd" as he called them, much as Ra now uses similar stones to control the people of this world.'

Mitac brightened. 'The stones are a focus for this power, then. It sends the instruction on an invisible beam.'

Kelly smiled at the young erfin. 'You are spot-on! You would make a great scientist, my little mate.'

Mitac returned the smile. 'And what does a scientist do?' he said.

'They are the ones who study the world and the cosmos. They solve the mysteries about everything,' Kelly replied.

'Yes, I wish to be this scientist you speak of,' Mitac said.

Ezof grimaced. 'I only wish to cut Ra into pieces and get this Einuk stone!'

'That will be difficult, my eager warrior friend. First let us get to the stone,' Kelly said.

Mirrortac rose. 'Then, take us there in your flying metal stone,' he said.

'Woo! Not so fast mate,' Kelly challenged. 'I'm not actually on government business now, so any attempt to take you on a plane will meet with a hell of a lot of opposition. I can't exactly tell them you're my hairy cousins from Transylvania ... and then there's the matter of passports. Not for furry aliens, I'm afraid.'

'Then we take your metal transporter,' the elder erfin countered.

'No can do. There's a whole ocean between us and Egypt. And we can't take a ship either.'

Mirrortac sighed. 'Then what? Why bother taking us here?'

Kelly's face brightened as he gave a sly smile. 'There are things that mere Earthlings don't know, but us Ancients do. They don't call us the masters of crystals for nothing. There is a cave not far from here with what humans would describe as a rich vein of Alexandrite. They do not mine it as there are sites far more accessible around the world. They know of some of its qualities, except as a stable means of transport once activated with the use of catalyst stones.'

'Then it acts like the Three Stones,' Mitac enquired.

'In some ways, yes,' Kelly explained. 'But only at short distances. And there is no need for protective headgear.'

'Then why do we stand here babbling? I itch to rid us of this Ra and his worrisome stones,' Ezof grumbled.

Mirrortac was lost in thought when he looked up at Kelly with a frown. 'Did you know all we spoke of that long day in that Egyptian quarry-teen? Did you know of all the worlds and how we lived?'

Kelly blushed. 'Yep, a fair bit, but not all. You filled in a lot of what I did not know.'

'Argh, all that chatter about matters that you already knew!' the erfin grumbled.

The Ancient went quiet, but a wry smile crept across his face.

EINUK ACTIVATED

Raul allowed himself a slight smile as he stared at the computer screen. Orders had streamed in for the 'Magical Egyptian Healing Crystal' and millions of people now foolishly hung it around their necks. The Astellite females had arrived carrying all the crystals that they had gathered, but Raul kept them out of sight in a building he had acquired only a few blocks away from the museum. At night, they busied themselves packaging the crystal orders that Raul sent off each morning to various addresses around the world.

A small stout man in a neat white robe entered the office and bowed. 'Your truck awaits, master. All has been arranged as you requested.'

'Good. You may go,' Raul answered with an abrupt wave of the hand.

The man bowed again and left.

'At last. I tire of all this nonsense. It is time for the real work to begin.' Ra filled a satchel with crystals and carefully packed the Einuk stone into a suitcase and made briskly for the truck parked at the back of the museum.

Soon he was travelling out of Cairo, past the pyramids and out into the desert. The truck rumbled along across sand and past limestone outcrops until, after many hours of travel, he reached an area of dunes where he came to a stop. The location was beyond sight of any road and all that could be seen were the peaks and troughs of sand parading across the desert landscape. Raul stepped out of the cabin and walked hundreds of metres away to a spot where he prostrated himself on the sand with arms outspread. He stayed that way for some minutes, seeming to feel vibrations from underneath before standing again and peering around him at the expanse of dunes.

Raul withdrew a large shadow amethyst crystal from a satchel he carried and placed it almost reverently on the sand where he had just lain. He then turned and began to count his steps for hundreds of metres until he reached a point where he deposited another crystal. He continued in different directions until there were four crystals laid out in a square equidistant from the central crystal. Finally, he returned to the truck and unfolded his turban, exposing the gleaming third eye of Ra. He used the turban again to wrap his nose and mouth until only his eyes peered out. Then, he took out one more crystal and began to mutter in a half-trance in a language that had not been uttered in thousands of years.

His golden eye shone, projecting into the crystal that he held out in front of him with his two hands. The crystal, in turn, sparked and fizzed to send out laser-like beams to each of the crystals spread out in the square ahead of him. The sand stirred as an unfamiliar wind rose over the pattern, coiling and twisting then rising in intensity until tonnes of sand were lifted in a blinding funnel that obliterated all vision of the surrounding desert. The storm soon overtook the area where he stood while he remained unmoved; not even his robe rustled in the violent torrent of sand and wind.

The storm raged for hours, gradually shifting to the south until the area around the pattern began to clear. It had gouged out a huge depression, exposing the top of something metallic that glared like silver in the afternoon light. Raul again unfolded the turban material from around his face and took out another crystal from the satchel. He spread out his arms wide and high and started muttering again in the ancient tongue.

The earth shuddered and groaned as though gripped in massive tremors before the metallic point began to ascend. Triangular sides rose out of the sand, revealing more and more of what appeared to be a massive pyramid of metal comprising innumerable small cells across its faces. The edifice continued to rise and expand until it dwarfed the width and height of the stone pyramids near Cairo to the east. Its summit was more like a mountain than any kind of structure as it dominated the sands for a great distance around.

Raul returned to the truck and gathered the suitcase with the Einuk stone. He peered back at the metal pyramid before striding towards it until he stood at the base of the nearest face where part of it projected out and formed a gleaming gold door with a pattern of symbols etched into its surface. He raised his hand to the symbols and ran his palm over the pattern until the door disengaged and he could open it. He stepped inside with the suitcase and immediately the door shut behind him. His third eye gleamed like a torch, revealing a long stairway ascending towards the centre of the pyramid. Raul disrobed then opened the suitcase. In a compartment below the Einuk stone were his golden robe and crown. He donned them then picked up the Einuk stone and began climbing with it up the steep stairs.

Crystal meridians ran equidistant up both walls and the ceiling of the stairway and lit up like stars as Ra almost floated up the stairs, leaving a deep darkness behind him as the glow of his third eye illuminated his path ahead. Finally, he reached the apex of the stairway where it levelled off into a spacious circular room. The meridians crossed the ceiling to a central structure where they met at an inverted pinnacle of metal capped with a large crystal above a pedestal.

Ra crossed to the pedestal and carefully placed the Einuk stone within it. The stone's shape slotted neatly into place, and suddenly it was as though a switch had been triggered. All the meridians lit up with an orange hue and the whole pyramid vibrated and hummed with power. The Einuk stone also lit up, accentuating the simple dark whirl pattern within. Ra placed the palm of his hand over the stone and smiled.

'My dear subjects. The mighty Ra calls you to service,' he intoned, his deep voice echoing in the chamber.

The meridians pulsed with millions of voices. 'We serve, and we obey!'

* * *

'What ails you,' Ameece said, frowning at Kelly.

Kelly groaned. 'Damn! Ra has activated Einuk. Nerthule will soon be under his control.'

'What do you mean?' Mirrortac quizzed.

'He has raised a power-grid ... a gigantic pyramid that amplifies the energy of Einuk and places all who wear his crystal stones to swear absolute allegiance to him. They will do anything he asks ... and I mean *anything*! We must tread with utmost care now.'

They had left the cabin and were following Kelly through a stand of conifers into the rising foothills and past granite outcrops and boulders. Mirrortac rubbed his leg as he struggled across the rough ground while Ezof and Treetam scrambled up nearby trees to get a better view of the way ahead.

The others halted as Kelly peered up at the two erfins high up in the tree. 'What do you see you two monkeys,' he jested.

Ezof glanced down and smiled. 'What did you call us?'

Kelly grinned. 'Monkeys ... they are creatures with tails that love to climb up trees. Some say they are related to us.'

Ezof nodded while Treetam stared off into the distance with wide eyes. 'I can see far across the woods at many mountains,' she said.

'Turn around. You should be able to see a cave up ahead,' Kelly instructed.

Ezof swung around and cleared away a branch that obstructed his view. His brows knitted together in concentration as he squinted up the slope. Then he beamed and spoke without looking down.

'Yes, I see the cave.' He pointed in a direction ahead of them. 'It is but a short way from here.'

Kelly shouted up to them again. 'That is where we are going now. Come down.'

Ezof and Treetam flipped down the trunk, leaping from branch to branch until they reached the others at the bottom.

'Impressive!' Kelly said, before starting off again.

The sun glinted through the trees as they made their way to a large rock outcrop that rose high above the trees. A musty cave entrance could be seen below a cliff face that supported the odd small shrub clinging tenaciously to the sparse accumulation of soil between the jagged rock. More trees grew at the top of the cliff above while moss and lichens grew profusely on the moist stone surfaces around the cave entrance. It reminded Mirrortac of his first encounter with a cavern when he took his people through the great mountain of Mateote while a blizzard turned the air outside into a blinding white mass. He was thankful that there was no blizzard this time as they approached the dark entrance.

Kelly ducked under the low ceiling of the cave as he led the way in. Stale air greeted them as they entered, and soon they were squeezing through a narrow opening into a black dank passage that stunk of bat droppings and insects. The erfins could see well but Kelly clutched at the walls and stumbled as he negotiated the pitch-dark surrounds. He muttered curses at his human eyes as his shoulder slammed into a sharp protrusion. The five followed with ease, although Mirrortac's rheumatism started acting up in the humid conditions. He winced as he raised his leg over the uneven floor and felt the cold smooth stone beneath the pads of his feet.

At last the twisting way opened into an area large enough for all of them to stand side by side. Kelly retrieved an object from his trousers and flicked it with his thumb. A small flame flickered up, illuminating the space and the walls where a torch could be seen attached to a metal support secured into the stone. Kelly lit the torch, which sputtered before bursting into a vigorous flame that lit up more of the cavern. He placed the small flame device into a pocket of his trousers and glanced around at the others.

'It is much easier from here now that I can bloody see,' he swore, then took the torch off the wall and began to make his way through the cavern and around a corner into another winding path with enough space to advance with ease.

The others followed in silence past drab stone walls until they began to see the odd sparkle of green and blue wink at them from out of the rock. Their shadows fluttered eerily behind them in the torchlight as they progressed through the passage. The cavern broke off into several smaller passages that veered off in various directions, and they were thankful that Kelly was confident in leading them the right way. Eventually, they entered a large cavern that sparkled with a string of green and blue Alexandrite veins that traversed across the ceiling and at various points along the walls.

'We're almost there,' Kelly advised, continuing past the gem deposits to another cavern where they were confronted with a man-size stone circle encrusted with Alexandrite that flickered green, blue and red.

'Is this the transportation portal?' Mitac blurted, his eyes wide and mouth agape at the extraordinary formation.

'Well spotted young Mitac,' Kelly replied. 'But you can't simply walk through it to another place. I will need to fire it up first.'

'Are you going to put the torch flame to it?' Mitac gasped, a little startled.

The Ancient laughed. 'Not exactly, my friend. I forget that you don't understand the looseness of my tongue. I meant that I will need to make some adjustments to activate the portal, then we can go through.'

'Oh ... best "fire it up" then,' Mitac said.

Mirrortac shook his head at the Australian's strange way of explaining things, while Ameece stared at the sparkling colours with some awe.

Kelly revealed several small crystals from his other trouser pocket and began to place them in grooves around the stone circle. He touched some random sites around the circle and shut his eyes in concentration. Mitac memorised each placement and scrutinised the structure with especial interest. Kelly was muttering something under his breath and kept this up for several minutes before he opened his eyes and took out another crystal to push it hard into a groove at the top of the stone circle.

There was a sudden bright flash of light that emanated from the crystals and the Alexandrite, filling the space inside with a dark opaque circle that flexed and vibrated with a glossy sheen.

Kelly gestured with his hand towards the pulsing circle. 'Pass through ... quickly now,' he said in an uncustomary abruptness.

Ezof did not hesitate as he rushed through and disappeared into the inky blackness. The others soon followed with Kelly last, and as he stepped through, he clapped his hands as he did so. They each felt a brief giddiness before being flung out into another cavern. The inky pool disappeared, allowing them to see through to the other side.

Kelly shivered as his body adjusted to the chill in the air of the cave. 'I hope that none of you are afraid of heights,' he said with a hint of a smile before striding off towards a glow of daylight at the edge of cavern.

They followed him again around into a short passage that opened into a sky with drifts of mist condensing into droplets at the edge of the opening. The five were taken aback when they reached the lip of the opening to discover they were an uncountable distance up on a cliff face.

Ezof hung out over the lip and peered down into the mist. 'Are we in the world of Egypt?'

Kelly glanced down then back at the erfin. 'Not quite. We have a long way to go to reach Egypt ... and we must pass through dangerous regions where men will shoot you and ask questions later.'

'Then you will not die,' Treetam stated.

'You surely will die, I'm afraid,' he replied.

'But then how can a dead one be asked questions?' she frowned.

'Oh, my loose tongue again. It is a saying for people who will kill you without giving you a chance to defend yourself.'

'Where are we then?' Mitac quizzed.

'We are in a region of the largest mountains on Earth, the Himalayas, in the north of a country called India and near the nations of Afghanistan and Pakistan.'

At that moment, the mist cleared to reveal a vista of snow-clad mountains rising to great heights across from them and joining onto the mountain that contained the cave system where they had arrived.

'How far is it to this country, Egypt?' Mitac asked.

'The distance is not the problem,' Kelly sighed. 'For us to avoid the trouble areas, we must go south to the Arabian Sea. There I can arrange for a boat to take us around to the Horn of Africa where we can travel to Egypt. We must travel only at night to avoid anyone seeing you.'

'But when we were back in the woods, you said we could not go by boat,' Mitac said.

'Not from America. The distance across the ocean is vast, but here the journey is short and the sea more protected ... and we can sail close to the coast all the way on a registered trading vessel.'

Mitac nodded. 'Let us "fire it up" then and move from this place.'

Kelly chuckled before approaching the lip of the cave and clambering over the edge until he hung and dropped out of sight. They all gasped before Kelly's voice echoed up at them.

'Take some care when you go over the edge. Slide down until you reach the ledge,' he cried out.

Ezof was again the first to move, but this time he was hesitant as he peered over the lip of the cave to the narrow ledge of rock below. He gingerly slid over the edge and down several metres until he landed beside Kelly. Mitac and Treetam went next, and then Ameece, before Mirrortac grunted and winced as he bent down to climb over. Soon, he also stood beside the others on the narrow ledge that hung precipitously over a sheer wall of rock descending into the valley below.

Kelly patted the elder erfin on the back. 'We'll take it slow down here. Just watch where I put my feet and follow exactly what I do, do you understand?' he glanced around at the others who all nodded their affirmation.

The ledge was part of a series of ledges and rock protrusions that led down the side of the cliff. Kelly clung to the rock face and stepped out along the ledge, then hopped down to the next ledge and followed it. Mirrortac and the others did as Kelly did, stepping and hopping onto the same spots as they progressed. At some points, they had to jump several metres across a gap, and despite Mirrortac's experiences with the tree-loving faugs, it made his knees tremble as there was no winged being to rescue him if he fell. Sometimes one of them would lose their footing and slip, but managed to climb back up to continue, thankful to their strong clawed fingers and toes in regaining a hold of the rock. A chill air made their fur ruffle in the wind, and sometimes they had to stop and wait as the area was blanketed in a fog that obscured the path ahead. The descent was slow and arduous, testing every muscle as they negotiated the unforgiving bare rock until they reached a series of man-made caves where they could rest before continuing.

It was already night by the time they had found the caves with their faded wall paintings. Scientists had long removed any artefacts from the caves as Kelly informed them, but even Mitac was too tired to examine the cave system further. They all fell into a deep sleep, not waking until a glimmer of sunlight shone up from beyond the mountains. The air outside was clear and dry with only the whisper of a breeze blowing across the rock face.

Kelly called out to them as they lay half asleep. 'We must go everyone. We'll have something to eat when we reach the bottom.'

He disappeared into the back of the cave and returned carrying a rope ladder that he threw over the edge and secured to ties bolted into the floor of the cave.

'It's much easier from here on. Come on, guys.'

The group dragged themselves up onto their feet and followed Kelly onto the ladder and down the last 20 metres to the boulder strewn ground where they negotiated a worn path into the valley still some distance below.

Mitac glanced back up the cliff beyond the caves and the drifting mists shielding the higher reaches from view. 'How do you go back this way to travel to America?' he asked, turning to Kelly.

'It is only one way from there ... no return ticket,' Kelly said.

* * *

They had trekked for several hours when Kelly took them to a lone hut on the side of a hill with the backdrop of snow-clad mountains contrasting with a lush green field of grasses and dainty flowers. A small man in a simple brown robe was milking a black-headed goat while other goats grazed freely on the grass near the hut. The man looked up and smiled as Kelly approached, and both embraced and exchanged greetings in a language none of the erfins had heard yet. They all immediately tasted the strong after-flavour of the faug essence as their ears adjusted to the new tongue.

The man regarded the erfins without any sense of surprise, but rather delight in his eyes and the tiny wrinkles around his lips. Kelly introduced him as Simeon of the Dropa and mysteriously glanced up with a small smile.

'Blessings on your celestial home and upon you.' Simeon bowed. 'Misser Kelly is much favoured in my house. We, like you, are visitors to this Earth. My ancestors arrived here from the sky but were unable to return.'

Mirrortac voiced the surprise expressed in his family's faces. 'We are from the world of Mareos and came here through a portal ... and it be our wish to return after we finish what we must do here,' he said.

Simeon looked up at Kelly then at the others. 'You came here through the Stones of Destiny? How can that be?'

Simeon became serious and contemplative before turning to Kelly. 'What is this about my friend? I dare not say what I think.'

Kelly shook his head from side to side. 'You got it right, Sim. The sarcophagus has been taken from the sea and Ra is resurrected along with the Einuk stone. This is the reason we are all here – we need to stop him before it is too late.'

Simeon stroked his small beard. 'How can I help, ancient one?'

'We must get to Egypt as soon as possible. We need clothing ... full coverings for my friends here, and food.'

'Of course,' the little man said, hastening into the hut and beckoning them all to follow.

Furnishings inside the hut were simple – a low table and cushions near a kitchen area where a stout small woman was busy preparing a bitter vegetable broth. A layer of straw in one corner constituted the couple's bedding.

The woman turned and smiled at the newcomers before offering some of the broth for all to eat. Curiously, she had made enough for all despite their surprise arrival. Simeon rummaged through an old chest and pulled out a bundle of clothing which he dumped on the floor.

'First, we will eat, then you can try out the clothes,' Simeon said.

After the meal, Kelly divided out the clothing and gave an item to each of the five. 'You will all be women for our purposes. These are traditional Islamic garments that will hide your furry parts. Hopefully none of those border guards will get a gander at your feet and hands ... but I can take care of that anyway.'

The robes were all white and easily draped over their frames. Black head coverings also hid their prominent ears and face, leaving only their eyes to betray them. Kelly also changed into more traditional garb, including a cloth wrapped around his head and draped around the sides of his face.

Kelly rubbed at the rough prickly whiskers on his face. 'Well, I hope this works or we're stuffed.'

'There will be a car waiting for you in the village near here. May your mission be a success,' Simeon said.

As Simeon promised, there was a car and driver waiting at the village where they took the road south. Sheets of fabric had been placed over the car's windows to obscure any view of the occupants, but the vehicle was old and prone to overheating, and had to make stops along the way for the radiator to cool and be replenished with water. The drive took several days through a landscape that transformed from the wooded mountain areas in the north to river flats with their grain crops and herds of bovine animals, goats and poultry. They noticed there seemed to be people everywhere, and many villages, towns and cities with their drab stone buildings and crowds. Many of the men were bearded while the women often hid their faces or covered their heads with basic shawls. The driver pushed slowly through the crowded streets, eventually leaving each town or city only to encounter more settlements further along the road.

Ameece signalled the driver to stop at a roadside market but Kelly wanted that to keep moving.

'Can't do the tourist thing here,' he said. 'Everyone will freak out when they see your furry feet.'

But Ameece was insistent. 'You can do this for me, James Kelly. Get the circlets at that place for me. We need enough for all of us.'

Kelly looked at where Ameece was pointing. 'You mean the market stall there? They sell bracelets, anklets and other jewellery ... pretty things.'

'Yes, whatever you call this small open house. I want the circlets for our legs ... big ones for us and a smaller one for you ... the blue ones,' she said.

Kelly manoeuvred himself out of the front seat as he opened the car door with a loud creak and strolled over to the roadside stall. He pointed out the anklets to the woman selling the goods and then pointed to the car. The woman nodded and approached the side of the car where Ameece was sitting. The driver reached back and cranked open the window enough for the woman to see Ameece's eyes under her dark head covering.

The woman showed Ameece a selection of anklets and looked surprised when Ameece selected some five oversized anklets and a normal-sized one.

'Do you have animals?' the woman asked.

'No. These are for us,' Ameece said.

The woman glanced back at Kelly who was standing nearby, and he nodded at her.

'Ahh, you like to make them go round and round?' the woman asked.

Ameece just smiled, which satisfied the woman who accepted some small slips of paper and round metal pieces from Kelly before returning to her stall.

Ameece noticed the woman pocket the curiously designed paper and metal pieces and tapped Kelly on the shoulder when he was again back in the front passenger seat.

'What be those parchments and metal medallions?' she asked.

'That is what we call money. We exchange it for items that we want from others. Everyone works … um, has specific tasks that we do in exchange for money which we use to buy things we need … food, clothes … jewellery and so on.'

Mirrortac and the others looked startled. 'That be a strange custom. You do not share your food with others? You must exchange for these bits of parchment and metal?' Mirrortac said.

Kelly seemed a little abashed. 'I am afraid that this is the way on this planet. If you do not have money, you have no home nor can you eat. It is regrettably how it is.'

The erfins were all surprised at this as was Ameece who looked clearly troubled.

'But we have none of this money of which you speak.'

Kelly waved dismissively at her. 'Do not worry. I will look after you all.'

Finally satisfied, Ameece muttered a maja blessing over the anklets as the driver again took to the road south. She handed them out to the others and Kelly who smiled at her as he accepted the gift. Mirrortac and the triplets immediately wore the anklets on their legs.

Kelly turned to her as he held up his anklet. 'And what does this do?' he said.

'It protects you from the evil ones,' she said.

Kelly nodded as he strung his anklet on his right leg in good faith.

Eventually, they made it into a port city on the coast of what Kelly called the Arabian Sea, and it was not until night that they slipped aboard a ship bound for the country of Somalia on the east coast of Africa. An almost complete moon lit up the sea with a shimmering reflection. Mirrortac lumbered aboard and immediately looked for any sign of creatures in the water to pull the boat but saw nothing. He remembered the Eeeps of the sea around the islands of the Meretees during his journeys on Mareos, and how these strong water creatures were tethered to the boats to pull them across the enormous expanses of water. The others glanced around at the water spreading out to the horizon.

'The lake is so … big!' Treetam gasped. 'It has flooded all that remains of Nerthule!'

'You would think so,' Kelly said. 'But like your Mareos, your vision cannot encompass all of the earth and its seas.'

Mitac glanced out at other boats and ships that sailed out into the sea under their own power, just like the cars on land. He wondered how the operators of these craft could steer through the constantly moving waters and the waves that made the craft lean from one side to another and front to back. And how did they know their way into the everlasting sea to the horizon? Some boats had canvas sails that used the wind to propel them, but those were smaller than the metal vessels that dwarfed them. Their ship was also of solid construction and of similar size to the larger of the sailing dhows.

Kelly was talking to a man in the control cabin at the stern while the others wandered around the cabin below them. Crew busied themselves on the large deck stretching out in front of the cabins. They loaded containers onto the deck and secured them while some worked with ropes to tie down items or attend to the mast towards the bow. The beast inside the hull chugged into life and spat grey smoke into the air through a pipe that jutted up from the back of the cabin area. The crew cast off the bollard ropes as the dhow crept out from the wharf and faced into the sea.

* * *

Kelly patted and rubbed Mirrortac's back as the erfin held a bucket in front of him. 'Feeling better mate?' he sympathised.

The erfin's white face peered out from under his black and white habit. 'I feel only the fluttering in my belly,' came the morose reply.

The bow ploughed deeply into the waves and came up with a splash of salt spray before wallowing sideways and coming down again.

'Still a few more days of this ... sorry,' Kelly ventured. 'Maybe we can stop off at Socotra. I'll have a word with the captain.'

Kelly disappeared into the upstairs cabin, and Ameece took his place beside him. She burped and looked away as the smell of the bucket contents wafted up at her.

'These waters test my own belly,' she reassured the elder erfin. 'I do not know how the triplets are so not affected.'

She gazed out the cabin window to where the triplets stood on the deck, swaying with the motion of the vessel.

'Perhaps it be like the trees that sway under their feet,' Mirrortac grunted.

Ameece sat beside him and comforted him, her blue irises staring out through the narrow slit in her robe hood. Kelly reappeared beside them and put his thumb up as a sign that all was well.

'Yeah, I've spoken to the the captain and he will be stopping at Socotra anyway. He has to drop off some cargo there. So, we can all take a break and you can stand on terra firma ... er, I mean solid ground, for a bit,' he grinned.

'And when will this be,' Mirrortac groaned, putting down the bucket.

'Oh, just a matter of hours now. Just hold on, hey. You'll soon be on dry land again.'

'Huh! It may as well be days,' the erfin spat.

'You two ought to get out on deck. Breathe in some of that fresh sea air. You'll feel much better, I guarantee,' Kelly promised.

Ameece stood up and grabbed Mirrortac by the arm. 'Maybe he is right. I can smell the breath of the dragon in here.'

Mirrortac clutched onto her as he slowly got up. 'If only these waters would be still for atime,' he said, staggering to his feet.

THE AWAKENING

Ra stood before a tightly fitting stone door in the deep bowels beneath the pyramid. He rubbed the sand and dust away from the face of the door until he revealed an indented hand shape and three hollow slots. He retrieved three crystals from a pocket in his robe and placed them in the slots. He placed the palm of his right hand into the impression and it fit perfectly.

'Open!' he commanded in the ancient tongue.

There was a rush of stale air as the stone door projected outward before grinding to one side.

'My dear friends, it is now time to awaken,' he said, stepping into the dark cavernous interior.

Ra shivered a little in the cold air as he strode into the darkness. Once he had walked some distance, it became apparent that it was not altogether pitch dark but illumined with an ultraviolet hue that created ghostly reflections off the stone walls and what appeared to be a gleaming lake in the centre of the huge cavern. When Ra moved nearer to the 'lake', its surface shimmered with a crystalline sheen, barely revealing numerous shadowy shapes beneath. The source of the black light came from a point directly above the crystal lake, somewhere high in the ceiling above.

Puffs of mist issued out of the demi-god's mouth as he stood at the edge and peered down at the many shapes within.

'Your long sleep has ended. I need you, my servants,' he whispered.

Ra placed both hands onto the crystalline surface and shut his two eyes while opening his third eye.

The eye shone with a bright razor light that pierced the translucent crystal, and his hands glowed a warm orange that radiated out across the surface. In seconds, the crystal lake turned into a fluid like jelly. Animal shapes rose out of the soup, dripping. The sounds of laboured breaths and rasping coughs filled the cavern as the forms twisted and stumbled with life. Thousands of these erect creatures dragged themselves through the gelatinous soup towards the one who summoned them.

'Come to me. The day has arrived for you to begin your work,' Ra encouraged.

One of the creatures came into view nearby and looked up with large wide eyes from a face and body covered in fur.

'Ah, one of my erfin collection. I have a special task for you and your brothers.' Ra glanced down at the being with a hint of a smile.

Other erfins and dark-skinned warrior men wearing leather skirts emerged out of the shadows.

'Master Ra, shining light of the East, we are at your command, great lord,' the many chorused.

* * *

Treetam shuddered despite the warm breeze. She sucked in the salty air and her hands trembled as she was suddenly reminded of the dark warrior men of Thenigmas. A stark vision of them in their mail shirts and short animal hide skirts came to her. She recalled the one carrying another man's head on a pointed stick, congealing blood streaming down and onto the ground. She recalled her rage as she obliterated every one of the warriors with the solar-bite, then realised her horror at what she had done. The sight of her brother and father about to be beheaded had been too much for her, and she had reacted out of desperation to save them. Bile rose up in her throat as she stood staring vacantly out at the rolling sea.

'What's wrong?' Mitac said as he noticed her fearful expression. 'Are you ill?'

Treetam shook her head and looked at her brother. 'No. I was just thinking about the warrior men I killed on Thenigmas. It still haunts me. I don't know why I thought of this now.'

Mitac nuzzled her shoulder. 'You saved Ezof and dada. You must forget about it.'

She sighed. 'I know. Why did I think about that now?'

Ezof grinned across at her. 'My sis the hero! I would do the same if it were you there.'

Treetam caught a thought from the air. 'Whatever ...?' she mused.

'Whatever!' the two brothers chorused. 'Where did that come from?'

Treetam allowed a slight smile. 'The tongue of the young ones of this planet. I can hear them in my mind. Their strange words come to me, and I like them.'

ATTACK ON KOSMO

Supreme Commander Sibuna paced his office as the chief maintenance officer stood at attention before him.

'You say we have only 50 ships prepared; how long before we can ready the other 150?' Sibuna queried, pursing his lips.

'We can have another 50 prepared for action in another two days, sir, but the remaining 100 are so badly damaged that we will need another two weeks to put another 50 on-line. Then there is the matter of renewing the laser arrays for warfare.'

The elder grunted and massaged his forehead. 'Is there no way to get these others armed and ready earlier? Bring in more labour. If we send those first 50 off now, then they will be outnumbered ... or we must try to pick those blasted tresoculi craft off guerilla style ...' Sibuna paused in thought.

The man waited in silence for some time before Sibuna looked up at him again.

'Get the 50 ready and start work on the others. Put a call out for more labour ... engineers, laser experts ... whoever you need. Work day and night until the ships are complete.'

'Yes sir,' the officer replied, turning and shaking his head when he was out of sight beyond the doorway.

Sibuna slumped back into his chair and sighed.

'Problems?' said a voice from out in the hall.

Wa-ku flicked a lever on his hoverchair and glided into the room. One shoulder was in a sling and a scar traversed one cheek.

'Don't talk to me about problems,' Sibuna growled, then glanced back at Wa-ku. 'So, I see you have your new chair. What do you think of it?'

'Much improved,' the golden-haired man beamed. 'I can go anywhere in this one. No need for metal guides.'

'Pleased to hear it, but I'm sure you didn't just come here for small talk. Out with it,' he ordered.

Wa-ku adjusted his sling as he swung the chair towards the desk. 'I want to be on the first flight out ...'

'Now, we already talked about this, Wa-ku. You are still on the mend,' Sibuna cut in.

Wa-ku manoeuvred the chair in an intricate show of movements before halting in front of the commander.

'I have only had this for a week. I've flown cosmo-ships for millennia,' Wa-ku boasted. 'Those erfins know me. They depend on me to get back to them.'

Sibuna shook his head. 'I can instruct one of the officers to rendezvous with the erfins. You are of much better use here.'

'Yeah, twiddling my thumbs,' Wa-ku growled.

Sibuna looked down at his desk then back at Wa-ku.

'Look, give it another week or so, maybe less, and I'll put you on the next fleet out. Will that satisfy you?'

Wa-ku paused while playing with the hoverchair controls, causing it to sway back and forth.

'Sure, okay. I'll accept that.'

'Good, now get out of my sight; I have work to do.'

'Right you are boss, I mean sir,' Wa-ku grinned, then added, 'I love this chair. Maybe that accident wasn't a bad thing after all.'

Sibuna grimaced. 'Now, don't you go wrecking that one. It cost big callugs.'

Wa-ku glided off down the hall and towards his quarters in the accommodation quarter, passing soldiers who guarded the various offices, dining, kitchen and private rooms. Security had been stepped up since the attacks by the Black Brotherhood, and camera drones scanned all areas. The destruction of any drone would immediately lockdown the area it patrolled and alert the nearest soldier post. Two soldiers stood either side of the door to his quarters as he approached, and saluted him as he input the remote pass code to open the door.

'All is secure, sir,' one soldier said, as the door swung open.

Wa-ku smiled politely to the soldiers as he entered the room and shut the door behind him. He hovered over to a monitor screen on the wall and pressed an icon on the digital touchscreen. It pulsed for a few moments before Hathor's face appeared on the screen. Her hair fell loosely over her shoulders as she smiled back.

'And how is my favourite patient doing?' she said.

'Couldn't be better. I may be needing a little of your bedside care,' he said, winking back at her image.

She blushed a little and twirled a finger through her locks. 'Hmmm, I'll have to see about that.'

'I have news. I will be flying out with the next fleet to Nerthule in about a week's time. I was wondering if I could see you before I head out?'

Hathor's eyes widened. 'Wa-ku, take me with you. I'd so love to see Nerthule!'

Wa-ku sighed. 'I'd love to, except this is no friendly visit. We will be at war with the Black Brotherhood … and there is more of them. It'll be too dangerous.'

Hathor pouted. 'I have already signed up for the medical corps to accompany the next fleet; you may as well have my company than for me to be on another ship.'

Wa-ku stared at the screen and frowned. 'Oh Hathor, I fear for you.'

Hathor looked at him sharply. 'It's just as dangerous for you, my blond Uranian. I'd rather for us to die together than to live without you.'

'Are you really sure about this? You want to be with me, even if it means death?' Wa-ku asked.

She nodded. 'I do … I um have become very fond of you.'

Wa-ku saw her eyes tear up before she turned her head away.

'Hmmm. I suppose a nurse on my crew could be advantageous.'

Hathor smiled with relief. 'I will take extra good care of you. You're my number one patient, after all.'

'I'm looking forward to that; perhaps we should get together and do a briefing before we go. Are you sure you can get assigned to my ship?'

Hathor's lips curled up in a cheeky grin. 'Oh, I'm sure. They have given me the pick of the fleet.'

Wa-ku threw his chin up and looked down his nose at her.

'You're one step ahead of me, then. My ship is the *Petrichor* and should be ready for the next fleet out.'

Hathor suddenly looked serious for a moment. 'Yes … the *Petrichor* will survive the calamity,' she said.

Wa-ku rolled his eyes and peered at her as if she had lost her mind. 'And you are now a seer, able to look into the future,' he mocked.

She shook her head and glanced sideways with a frown. 'No … I don't know where that came from. It just came out.'

'Well, let's hope you're right, my dear.'

* * *

Yidu frowned at the body of the woman on the bed. He glanced around at the other tresoculi with him and scowled. 'How did this happen? Did you use too much serket toxin?'

A man in a white medical robe shook his head. 'She was stable till a day ago, then she suddenly deteriorated.'

'Maru was to be awakened yesterday. How convenient! As if the old witch knew what we were planning for her. No matter, Ra is already on the ascendant. The fleet will have Nerthule prepared before any of those incompetent duoculi can do anything about it.'

'Shame. She was the only living Ancient left,' One of the officers lamented. 'Who will look into the Pool of Knowledge now?'

Yidu snarled. 'Not the last Ancient living,' he said. 'Nerthule has a guardian for the Einuk stone, I believe. But who it is not even Ra knows ... yet.'

The medical man regarded the greying body and frowned. 'So, master, what do we do with her now that she is dead?'

'Lay her at the entrance to the halls; let the two-eyes take care of it,' Yidu said with a dismissive wave. 'We have more important matters to consider now. We must prepare to give the two-eyes another reminder of who's in charge. Once you have dropped the body off, we will prepare to attack the centre.'

* * *

A funeral pyre had been set up in the memorial courtyard outside the Halls of Ra where Maru's body lay on a timber bed suspended atop a hollowed stone slab filled with a flammable liquid. Her simple green robe covered her body. The five duoculi of the inner council stood with glum faces at the base of the pyre structure while many of the representatives of the various provinces filled the courtyard along with a crowd of people who lived and worked in the capital. A ring of soldiers surrounded the crowd. Wa-ku adjusted his chair into a hover beside Hathor and near Sibuna who was preparing to address the crowd.

Sibuna cleared his throat as he looked up from a dais set up nearby.

'My dear brethren and sisters of Kosmo, it is my sad task to take on what normally is the job of an Ancient, but as we have no Ancient alive at hand, then I must lead us in our farewell of our great and Ancient sister Maru who has guided us for the past 30 millennia. Maru has been taken from us at a time of apostasy in which our universal principles have been betrayed. She sacrificed her life to guard the secrets revealed in the Pool of Knowledge, and thus foil the attempts of these traitors who seek to commit the unforgivable upon our subject guardian peoples. Maru has risen to be among her sisters and brother Ancients until such time that she may seek to walk among us again in a new body.'

Sibuna nodded to one of his inner chamber members who prepared to press the ignition crystal at the base of the structure.

'We now call upon the Ancient Werd and the Universal Master to sanctify Maru-the-Green's holy journey into the mists beyond time and space and dismiss this bodily vessel of any obligation and return it to the ashes of existence from which it arose. Oh great and holy be the Werd!' he proclaimed.

'Great and holy be the Werd,' the crowd repeated.

The inner chamber member depressed the ignition crystal, and a clear flame flushed up from the slab beneath Maru's body. The timber bed started smoking then burst into flame which soon overwhelmed the body in a cleansing fire that rose high into the air. Sibuna watched with tears trickling down his face as the bed collapsed onto the slab and the body slumped and dissolved in a ball of fire that briefly distinguished its shape before it disintegrated entirely.

The crowd bowed their heads in silent respect as the flames died down and smouldered into ashes. Hathor looked up at the sky above the pyre and nodded to herself as though coming to some understanding.

'I think Maru is not far from us. I believe she is still looking out for us,' Hathor said, looking into Wa-ku's eyes.

Wa-ku gave her a worried glance. 'I don't know if she can help us any more. The sooner I can get back to Nerthule, the better.'

'You will have to go to Mareos first,' Hathor piped up.

'Why do you say that?' he asked, a little confused.

'To pick up the two other Stones of Destiny before you go to Nerthule.'

Wa-ku pulled back, a little startled. 'I have never mentioned the stones to you. Where did you hear about them? How do you know that two stones are now on Mareos?'

Hathor shrugged. 'I just know. Funny that ... where did I get that from?'

Wa-ku looked askance at her and eyed her dubiously. 'Are you only pretending to be a nice caring nurse or are you some sort of spy? You are really making me wonder.'

Hathor pouted. 'A spy? No! I can't explain where this comes from. I'm as confused as you are.'

She looked around with nervous agitation. 'Come on. We've got to get out of here.'

'What's the hurry?' he said.

Hathor grabbed his hand and pulled him after her. 'I don't feel safe. Come on!'

He fell in beside her as she strutted across the pavement towards the ring of uniformed men and women at one end of the courtyard. They jostled through people as Hathor hastened them out beyond the assemblage. There was a disturbance near the halls as a bright flash discharged. The ground trembled and several soldiers disintegrated into acrid piles of ash. The other soldiers immediately swung around and threw up their clear crystal shields. People screamed in panic and stampeded away from the affray.

Wa-ku gaped at Hathor. 'You knew? How?'

She returned a pleading look and shrugged.

'Get on!' he commanded.

'What do you mean get on?' She glanced back confused.

'Get on my lap. This chair moves faster than you can run.'

'Will it hold the both of us?'

He nodded with agitation. 'Just get on.'

She sat back on his lap, and as her feet left the ground, he accelerated down the boulevard. They left the mayhem of people running for their lives as soldiers battled to stave off the attack. Wa-ku felt his stomach turn as the familiar smell of burnt flesh wafted up in the breeze. He dared not look behind as the cries and explosions betrayed the slaughter that beset the memorial courtyard and the halls. Wa-ku pushed the throttle to its maximum as he recalled the battle at the plant nursery. He held his breath as he half expected to be blasted but the noise of the fight diminished behind them. Hathor wrapped her arms around his neck and kissed him tenderly on the side of his forehead as they made their escape.

In their aimless rush, they found themselves in the central city area. Hathor touched Wa-ku on the shoulder and pointed to a side street.

'My quarters are just a few blocks away down there,' she said.

Wa-ku flicked the controls to the right into the street and eased back the speed. He only then realised that his heart was thumping with the adrenaline and his knuckles were pale from gripping the throttle control. They passed a series of domes and intersections before Hathor told him to turn into a lane.

'Third one down,' she indicated.

They halted in front of a modest unit with a pastel pink doorway. Hathor leaped to her feet and strode up to the door. She pushed her hand against the keypad, and the door opened.

'I wasn't expecting you over just yet.' She turned around and gave him a shy smile. 'I wish it was in better circumstances.'

Wa-ku glided into the entrance and let out a breath. A nursing bag had been tossed on a sofa near the doorway, and unwashed uniforms lay in a heap on the floor. Hathor pressed a button on the curved white walls, and a kitchen revolved out of part of the wall, complete with a dining bar, fridge, stove and flush cabinets.

'Make yourself comfortable ... oh, just perch yourself somewhere.' She eyed the hoverchair and waved her arm at the lounge room. 'I'm getting us something to steady the nerves. I don't know about you, but I certainly need it.'

Hathor's hands were shaking as she opened a cabinet and produced a bottle and two tumblers.

'You'll find this the best medicine around for high anxiety.' She poured a dark liquid into the tumblers and offered him one.

Wa-ku accepted the drink while staring at her.

'How long have you had this ability?'

Hathor sat down on a nearby chair and twisted her lips. 'Ability?'

'You know what I mean. This ability to sense things, third eye stuff?' He leaned towards her and raised an eyebrow.

She gulped the soothing liquid and peered down into her lap. 'I've never been able to do ... sense before. It only started a few days ago. It's like someone is showing me things in my mind.'

'Extraordinary. You realise you just saved our lives.'

Hathor swept up a hand to her eyes and burst into tears.

'What is going on? They are killing their own people!'

Wa-ku manoeuvred up to her chair and placed his hands on her knees to comfort her. She clutched his hand and looked into his eyes.

'I'm frightened for our people. The three-eyes are betraying everything that the Universal Guardians stand for.'

Wa-ku regarded the moist brown eyes and her tear-stained dimples.

'It seems this has been a long time in coming, and we have been ignorant of the three-eyes' plans for power. I thought Yidu's ravings were mere old tales of our great uncle Ra. I'm afraid I have only served to aid my brother in his revolt.'

'You did what anyone should do, Wa-ku,' she said, then she raised her eyes to him as a thought came to her. 'How did two brothers come to be so different?'

Wa-ku sighed. 'I too was consumed by the power game not so long ago. But my brother always thought himself superior, being a tresoculi ... they have ... "abilities". He was my great uncle Ra's favourite. Ra groomed him and set him against me. I was glad when Ra "died", or at least I thought he had died. I was so wrong ... Ra is more diabolical than I ever realised. Yidu is the only three-eye in several generations of my family, since Ra; and my great uncle saw the opportunity and grabbed it. He corrupted my brother.'

Hathor sniffled and took a sip of her drink. 'There were no three-eyes in my family. We did have an Ancient but that was, like, way way back.'

'Hmmm, I think some of my cousins had relatives who were Ancients, but I never met any of them,' Wa-ku said.

The two discussed their families and the evening's attack as they finished the bottle and ate some snacks, until the communication monitor on the wall buzzed. Hathor flicked her fingers to turn it on. The hospital matron's grim face materialised.

'Yes matron, do you need me?' the young woman quizzed, immediately adopting her nursing mode of address.

'Please come over right away. We have wards full of injured from tonight's attack. I need everyone I can get.'

Hathor stood upright and glanced around at Wa-ku with apology in her eyes. 'I have to go. Promise you will stay here. I doubt it will be safe at the halls. Get some rest ... the extra bed is the blue button there.' She pointed at a group of buttons on the wall near the kitchen.

Wa-ku waved an arm dismissively. 'Go. I'll be okay here. I'm feeling kind of tired anyway.'

Hathor opened her room and hastily gathered a uniform from a wardrobe, then cast off her clothing without regard for the man in clear sight in the other room. Wa-ku tried not to look but could not resist glimpsing the smooth white skin and curves beneath her scant underwear. She hastily donned her uniform and glanced back with a hint of a cheeky smile.

'Don't wait up for me,' she said as she raced to the door and disappeared into the street.

Wa-ku felt a warm flush come over him. Perhaps it was the intoxicating nature of the drink, he thought.

* * *

It was nearly sunrise when he felt the bed creak as a weight bore down beside him and slung a slim arm over his chest. He was too drugged with sleep to respond except to welcome the warmth of the woman's body cuddling up to him. She too, was exhausted, and soon fell asleep holding him.

It was nearly the middle of the day when Wa-ku awoke and twisted himself around to see Hathor lying alongside, wearing only her panty. He admired her natural beauty and the soft shooshing of her breath as she slept. He mused about this shy and caring being's new ability. It seemed more than a little coincidental that she had developed it at this crucial time of what amounted to civil war. He ran his finger over her face and along her thick lips, and those lovable dimples that were so pronounced when she laughed.

With regret, he flung his legs over the side of the bed and into the hoverchair. After what had happened the night before, he dreaded but needed to know the news of what happened to those in the memorial courtyard. Had the elders survived? And what of Sibuna? He approached the monitor and pushed in the code for Sibuna's office, then held his breath.

'Wha... you doing dear?' came a drowsy voice from behind him.

Wa-ku looked back at the bed. Hathor's eyes were looking up at him, but her lids were still heavy with sleepiness.

'Go back to sleep, love. I need to find out what's happening. I'm calling Commander Sibuna.'

The woman reached out her hand. 'Come here. You can find that out later.'

Wa-ku curbed his desire and turned back to the screen in time to see the grey-haired elder appear.

'Oh, thank the Werd, you're okay,' he spluttered.

Sibuna appeared haggard. 'And I am glad to see you escaped with your life too,' the elder said. 'We took a heavy toll. My officers ensured that we elders were safely removed from the fighting, but I'm afraid many paid with their lives. We lost a lot of civilians too. Though we did succeed in taking some of the brotherhood down and push them back to their demon holes.'

'Did they get at the ships?'

'No. Their attack was concentrated on the city. But I fear they will target our ships next ... and that is why I will be sending the fleet out tonight, and you will be with them.'

Wa-ku brightened. 'At last! I will be ready.'

'But you must not engage the enemy if possible. However, if in the event that you come under attack, I am stationing two plasma gunners under your command.'

Wa-ku flicked his head back to the woman who now stared back at him from the bed.

'Ah sir, Hathor will also be on my ship. She has joined the nursing contingent accompanying our fleet.'

A glint came to the elder's eyes. 'I know. I saw her name on your ship's crew list. I'm sure she will ... take good care of you.' One side of his mouth edged into a smile.

Wa-ku blushed slightly as he smiled back. 'Yes, if you say, sir.'

'He is in good hands,' Hathor shouted out, grinning.

Sibuna's smile had widened now. 'As I can already see,' he said, winking. Then his face turned serious again. 'Be at the fleet station at 1800; and make sure you get there safely. I want you to save that foolhardy erfin friend of yours before Ra reduces him to dust.'

Wa-ku bowed at the screen. 'Yes sir! The erfin and his family have been my concern for some time now.'

Sibuna also bowed. 'Good! Prepare yourselves, both of you.'

The screen went to black and Wa-ku turned back towards Hathor who cast a cheeky eye up at him.

'Now come here my big boy. We still have some time for ...' her voice trailed off as her lithe arm reached out and invited him back to the bed.

* * *

Wa-ku and Hathor found the cosmo-ship fleet station heavily guarded as they entered through the security entrance. A uniformed woman ran a scanner over each of their arms where their ID implants verified their identities and matched them with the authorised personnel for that night's fleet departure.

The woman bowed her head at them and pointed down a wide corridor. 'The *Petrichor* is prepared at Gate 36, sir. Just proceed down this corridor and you will find it.'

Wa-ku nodded a quick thanks and transported them on his hoverchair to the gate where his ship had been prepared. Two soldiers were waiting at the gate and bowed as Wa-ku approached. They introduced themselves as Cibell and Thar-karn the plasma gunners. Cibell was a short man with long orange hair tied up in a pigtail at the back of his head, and a moustache that fell in long strands to either side. Thar-karn had curly blond hair like Wa-ku and was tall, thickset, and clean shaven. They led the way to the gate where a man in a light blue uniform again scanned their arms before handing Wa-ku a digital tablet with the orders for his part in the mission. He then unlocked the gate door allowing them access to the cosmo-ship.

Wa-ku looked up at the *Petrichor* as they entered the large hangar. He noted there had been some modifications – twin plasma guns had been incorporated at the front and back and could swivel in a 360-degree arc for maximum targeting efficiency, and were retractable within the body of the ship when not in use. The portal boosters had also been upgraded to overcome some handicaps experienced with the older ships. Once they were inside, he could also see the docks for the gunners, and extra screens and instruments for locating and targeting, shielding and manoeuvring at supersonic speeds. Wa-ku took a long breath as he contemplated the realities of war and the possibility they would encounter tresoculi resistance. Cibell and Thar-karn took up their positions in the gunning docks while Hathor checked the medical supplies. Wa-ka docked his chair in position at the control array and started the pre-flight checks.

The hangar gate slid open, revealing clusters of stars and constellations twinkling in a clear evening sky. Wa-ku inserted the digital tablet into a slot below the screen and pressed the 'on' button. The crystals sparkled then formed into the shape of the Supreme Commander. The elder's voice boomed into the interior, immediately gaining the attention of everyone in the ship.

'Captain Wa-ku and the crew of the *Petrichor*,' Sibuna began. 'It is with heavy heart that I send you into the war with the tresoculi traitors flying to the aid of Ra. I do not send you off as frontline combatants but as a specialised support team for the erfins on the hunt for the final Stone of Destiny, Einuk. It is folly for such primitive beings to take on the power of Ra, and despite their incredible success against Yidu, I have doubts as to this mission. That is partly why they will need your support, including assisting their escape with or without the stone. It is also your mission to locate the Ancient now residing on Nerthule before the tresoculi find him or her. Should they access the Pool of Knowledge, all our futures could be in grave danger. Maru died protecting us ... we do not want to lose another Ancient. The triad of the worlds' alignment is soon at hand, and Ra must not gain hold of Nerthule. My understanding is that you will pick up the other two stones at Mareos on your way, but I urge you to waste as little time as possible there as your prime objective is to get to Nerthule as quickly as you can. May the holy Werd guide you and see you back safely.'

Wa-ku glanced around at his crew with a sigh. 'Well this is it, people. Let's be on our way.'

Hathor sat beside him and rubbed his shoulder. 'We'll be fine.'

Wa-ku swung around in his seat and flicked several switches. A hum rose from the engines, propelling the craft a short distance off the floor. 'Now, let's see what we can do with *Petrichor* in its improved state,' he said as the ship drifted towards the opening.

'Belt up people!' he shouted, and immediately everyone secured themselves into their seats.

When the ship had drifted outside the opening, Wa-ku pushed a lever forward, thrusting them instantly into space at such a rate that the light from all the stars merged into a white blob covering the whole viewing screen. Hathor gasped as she was momentarily crushed into her seat before the gravity inducers kicked in and stabilised the G-forces that would otherwise kill them at such a speed.

When she regained her breath, she stared back at him with wide eyes. 'Wow! I can't wait to see Mareos and Nerthule. What an adventure!' she cried.

Behind them, Kosmo diminished into a tiny dot before disappearing in the vastness of it all. Cibell and Thar-karn were acquainting themselves with the plasma gun controls while Hathor blinked at the white blob and the navigation screens with their moving points representing suns, planets and other space matter. She saw a cluster of points marking other cosmo-ships diverge from their path and go off screen while the *Petrichor* continued towards Mareos.

The communication screen burst into life as Fayth smiled at them from the operations room at Kosmo. 'Captain Wa-ku sir, good to see you again,' she quipped.

'And you Fayth. What have you got for me?'

'You're coming up to the Mareos sub-portal sir. Your ship is now equipped to negotiate it, but I do suggest that all your crew ensure they are well secured. Move to sector 7547 at Nav. 890.2809850 and engage your portal boosters no sooner than the first break point. Then hold on for a wild ride.'

Wa-ku looked back at the screen with some hesitancy. 'Are you sure we can handle it, Fayth?'

Her eyes glinted as she grinned back. 'I'm sure you'll be all right, sir. Of course, we don't know for sure how the ship will react,' she teased.

Wa-ku's face paled as he forced a smile. 'Always the kidder aren't you Fayth?'

'Hey, comes with the job, sir.'

Her face disappeared into black as the navigation point for the sub-portal loomed up.

'You all heard her. Make sure you're belted up tight,' Wa-ku said, catching the worried look in Hathor's eyes.

He took her hand in his and clasped it tight as the ship reached the point that Fayth had indicated. There was a giddy slide as they shot into the sub-portal and Wa-ku engaged the portal boosters. Hathor grabbed hold of him as she tried to focus her eyes but found she couldn't. They were all having the same problem as everything became a blur of changing shapes and colours. Wa-ku removed his other hand from the controls and let the ship be taken along through the winding cosmic pathway that now swirled them through space, cutting the time it would normally take to travel the distance to Mareos. Wa-ku held Hathor close as her face danced in jarring shades in front of his eyes. There were moments when she seemed to change form into some other woman and a golden light sparked around her head. Sinister spectres floated across the interior while they felt vibrations that made their teeth chatter and stomachs turn and flutter like nervous insects. The hallucinations and shuddering seemed to go on forever until finally the ship shot out of the sub-portal and stabilised.

Wa-ku turned off the portal boosters and sunk back into his chair. He and Hathor rubbed their eyes as they regained focus and recovered from the dizziness and nausea.

Thar-karn shouted out, 'Woohoo! That's the best one I've been on so far!' and let out a big belly laugh.

Cibell was also grinning and chuckling. 'Yeah! What a doozy!'

Hathor slumped into Wa-ku's shoulder. 'Are they kidding? I hope there's no more of these portals.'

Wa-ku nodded in agreement. 'I will second that, my dear.'

Wa-ku slowed the ship until the screen view showed a planet dead ahead. They cruised closer with Hathor's eyes now glued to the vision of Mareos with its seas and various landforms. The blond Uranian flew the ship towards the northern hemisphere and nearer the polar ice-cap. A flush of yellow flames lit up around the ship as it entered the planet's atmosphere and descended below a layer of cirrus clouds to reveal an icy tundra landscape and a mesa covered in snow. A palace, half in ruins, appeared, and a thin stream of smoke issued from one of the crystal flutes on its roofline. Wa-ku landed in a clear flat area to one side of the palace and shut down the engines.

'What is all that white stuff?' Hathor enquired.

'Here they call it the White Veil, but on Nerthule it is known as snow,' Wa-ku explained, disengaging his hoverchair and opening the hatch to the exterior.

Hathor sucked in a breath as a cold breeze entered the interior of the ship. She was suited up, but the cold air gave her goosebumps on her arms.

'Oooh, the white stuff – the snow – is cold and wet,' she said as she strode out onto the ground outside and peered at the palace behind.

'It is the crystal form of water. We have it in the highlands on Kosmo.'

Hathor scrunched her hand into the snow and formed it into a ball shape. 'Why hadn't I known about this before. It's delightful, but so very cold.' She dropped the lump and massaged her bare hand.

Wa-ku smiled. 'It's best handled with thick gloves.'

Cibell and Thar-karn ventured out and were also examining the snow.

'I have heard of such,' Cibell commented. 'I have only seen it from up high.'

A big furry being emerged out of one side of the palace and approached them.

Wa-ku smiled up at the hyfnuk. 'Ah, Evarngar, we have need of the two stones.'

Evarngar lifted a hairy brow and stared towards the cosmo-ship. 'Where is my mistress and Mirrortac? Have you not brought them back from that other world? I have heard naught from them nor you since they were sucked into that sky hole.'

Wa-ku became solemn. 'I have no knowledge of Mirrortac and his kin's movements on Nerthule, except that we hope he has met with the Ancient one who is guardian of the last Stone of Destiny. We must be in haste as Ra is gaining power and there has been a rebellion on our world in his support.'

Evarngar frowned. 'Then it be as I fear. How be it that such god-men as yourselves meddle with our lives!'

He swivelled around and stomped back towards the palace. 'Come then and claim your retched stones.'

Hathor marvelled at the hyfnuk as he withdrew before she sat on Wa-ku's lap as he led them all towards the palace.

'What a curious creature,' she said, not intending any disrespect. 'Our kind have much to answer for.'

Wa-ku felt a twinge of guilt as they glided over the snow followed by the two gunners.

Evarngar led them through a gap in the side of the building into the main hall. The master Werdstone remained firm in its pedestal next to a gem-encrusted throne above a platform with steps leading onto the soft matted gemstone floor. Behind the platform and at the confluence of a crystalline chute descending from the roof was a large ceramic bowl that served as a fireplace. Within it were thick blocks of wood that burned with a healthy flame and warmed the area in its vicinity.

Wa-ku surveyed the palatial surrounds with a sneer. 'So, this is where my brother lavished himself in the luxury of his godliness.'

The gunners peered open-mouthed at the gems, marblelite and exquisite crystalline aesthetics of the building that they admired despite the shambles of broken and leaning pillars, and holes in the roof structure and walls.

Evarngar was clearly in no mood for jest as he led them past the throne and the fireplace into a side corridor, grunting and glaring back at them with pursed lips. He finally entered a side chamber where the two stones – Oashu and Darm – were firmly locked together, leaving one curved side for the remaining stone of Einuk.

Thar-karn glanced back at Wa-ku and motioned to Cibell to follow him. 'We'll get it sir, with your permission?'

Wa-ku nodded for them to go ahead.

The men picked up the combined stones, and found they had to use both hands to carry it as it was surprisingly heavy.

Hathor was staring at the two stones as though lost in thought. 'These will guide you to Einuk and the Nerthulian Ancient,' she announced.

Wa-ku looked sideways at her, stunned. 'How would you know this, Hath?'

'I know it as though it were taught to me as a child. Strange that,' she mused.

'And how does it work, then?' Wa-ku quizzed her.

Hathor inclined her head as she considered his question, then she looked up with bright eyes. 'The dark curls will begin shining ... the joining pattern ... phew! What is that!?' She shook her head in amazement at her own words.

Wa-ku rolled his eyes at her. 'Okay, who are you?'

Hathor shrugged and gave a nervous chuckle. 'Just a nurse ... I'm just a nurse,' she pleaded.

'A nurse who seems to know about things that only the elders and Ancients know. A nurse who can sense danger. Come on, who are you really?'

Hathor stood up and her eyes flared back at him. 'I'm telling you the truth, Wa-ku. I have no idea where this is coming from, but I know in my heart it is true. Stop doubting me!'

Hathor stormed off through the corridor, leaving Wa-ku alone with Evarngar who was giving him a puzzled look.

'Go and find my mistress and the erfins,' Evarngar said with a dismissive wave.

'I don't know what to make of this, Evarngar. I best be off then.'

Wa-ku cringed into his chair and set it in motion down the corridor.

Back at the ship he was in for another surprise as he found them all staring at the Oashu-Darm stone with their mouths agape.

'What now?' he mouthed with some irritation in his voice.

When he looked down at the stone, the pattern was glowing a rich golden hue. He glanced over at Hathor who squatted down beside the stone and gently rubbed her hand over the patterns.

'Ed lumen du mort,' she whispered, and the pattern returned to its black colouration.

Suddenly it all made sense to him. 'Oh Hathor, great and holy be the Werd within you.' His eyes teared up as he wore a quivering smile.

She turned to him with incomprehension then realisation also struck. 'Could it truly be? Me ... just a nurse,' she said, shaking her head lightly to deny what she knew to be true.

'An Ancient has chosen you as a vessel, Hath. You must let go to it. All of the wisdom will come to you gradually,' he encouraged.

Tears were also streaming down her face. She was shaking as she threw herself into his arms and wept into his shoulder. 'I am so sorry to run out on you like that. Please forgive me.'

'No sweetheart. It should be I who must apologise. I should have known; I should have seen the signs.'

Hathor kissed him on the cheek then fully on his mouth before collapsing back into his arms again.

'Er ... umm,' Cibell interrupted. 'Sir, we have a mission to complete. Time is of the essence.'

Wa-ku wiped his face with his hand. 'Yes, yes, it is not every day that a new Ancient is realised. Start preparing; we will be along in a moment.'

He cupped Hathor's face in his hands and smiled through his tears. 'You are a wonder my sweet. It is an honour to be at your side.'

Hathor blushed as she looked up into his blue eyes. 'The honour is mine my love.'

MEETING WITH ERFINS

irrortac and Ameece strolled along the island street where they passed dark-skinned people who wore shirts and skirts and wrapped their heads in cloth, showing their faces, and sometimes their unkempt black hair. The erfin and the roznogh kept themselves well disguised in their white robed outfits as they traversed the dusty street lined by flat-roofed clay coloured buildings. Black thick threads were suspended on T-shaped poles and linked the buildings. There was no tree to be seen but they recalled the curious mushroom shaped trees they saw from the boat as they had approached along the island's coast. Kelly had called them dragon blood trees, and they wondered if such a creature's blood fed the roots of these arborial wonders.

Kelly appeared from farther down the street and waved at them but said nothing until he came up to them. 'They've finished loading so we will need to make our way down to the dock and board the boat. Are you feeling better my friend?' he said.

Mirrortac grimaced. 'A little better but the land has not yet steadied under my feet.'

The Australian smiled despite the erfin's discomfort. 'Yeah ... the sea does that to you. You'll be right if you don't look down too much. Just stay out on deck. The sea's not too rough today.'

Mirrortac limped along behind as Kelly led them back to the dhow. Ameece held his arm and supported him as the rheumatism in his leg made walking difficult. The triplets emerged from the beach as they approached, after having relished walking in the sand and shallows along the shoreline. They laughed and danced without any sign of sea sickness, which brought a small smile to the elder erfin's lips. The day seemed perfect on this island world from another time – the sun was shining, and the sea was a shimmering turquoise with no sediment, thus revealing the white sand below and the fish whose silver scales reflected up as they swam.

Kelly fingered the stone on his neck as they boarded the boat, but his face became creased and solemn as his grey-blue eyes turned towards the sea.

The erfins ambled aboard in their white robes, revealing only their eyes as they swept up the gangplank and onto the deck like phantoms. Kelly rushed past them and up to the wheelhouse where he engaged in an animated discussion with the captain who then turned around and instructed the crew to cast off immediately.

Ropes were hastily undone from the bollards on the wharf and the mooring lines secured on the ship. No sooner had this happened when the motor chugged into life with accompanying puffs of smoke as the vessel eased away from the dock. Kelly seemed to be gesturing to the captain as to the heading, while the bearded man seemed to disregard the Ancient. In the distance was another vessel steaming rapidly in their direction, and it seemed to Mitac that they were trying to avoid the other ship.

Soon, the others also noticed it. 'They're chasing us,' Treetam said, frowning.

Ameece turned to Mirrortac. 'Who would these be who pursue us? None know of us or our purpose here.'

'Ra knows where we are,' a voice came from behind them.

Kelly appeared agitated. 'It's this stone.' He fingered the gemstone on his neck again. 'Once Ra activated all his little slave stones, he could track us. Anyone wearing them will do as he asks. I'm guessing these are pirates.'

'Why did you not cast away your stone?' Mirrortac queried.

Kelly sighed. 'I have been using it to track Einuk, but I did not think about it tracking me ... us.'

'Then Ra knows you are with us ... that you are an Ancient?' Mitac surmised.

Kelly shook his head with shame. 'It would appear so, fellas. I have been gone too long, so he just put two and two together.'

They all looked at him confused.

'I mean, he was able to work it out that I am with you ... or perhaps,' he mused, 'he wants access to me in my capacity as an Ancient.' He slapped his forehead. 'Oh shish! Damn! The Pool of Knowledge ... of course!'

'Pool ... of knowledge?' Mirrortac looked puzzled.

'The Pool of Knowledge is in the spirit world. It can look into the future, but only we Ancients can go there.'

Mirrortac fixed Kelly with a dirty look. 'Oh, so wise are the Ancients,' he snarled.

The Australian just nodded. 'Knowledge is not wisdom, it is true. The wisdom is in the beyond I'm afraid.'

Mitac shot a glance at the approaching ship then back at Kelly. 'We need weapons. If these are Nerthulians, then we can defeat them.'

'Love your confidence, little mate, but we have no weapons on board, and even if we did, I'd bet we would be no match for these guys.'

The dhow picked up speed and began purposely steaming towards the other ship, which was also a large vessel.

Kelly swore. 'Silly bugger. He wants to ram them!'

Mirrortac watched the bow plunge down into the waves, sending salt spray up on the forward deck before lurching up again as they progressed onward. He held on to a nearby railing as the ship rolled before plunging down again.

Ezof let out a cry and punched his fist into the air at the other vessel.

'Yes! Smash them!' he shouted.

Kelly was not so amused. 'I suggest you all put on your life vests. Take off your robes. We may all be going for a swim if this lunatic ends up sinking this boat.'

'Do you make amusement? Swim! Out in that wet?' Mirrortac was trembling.

'No joke, mate. But let's hope it doesn't come to that.'

Kelly swung back and stomped off towards the captain's cabin, cursing and waving his arms as he went.

Ameece comforted the erfin but was biting her lip at the unfolding drama. The triplets quickly cast off their robes and donned their life vests but Mirrortac and Ameece still stared out at the pirate vessel that abruptly changed direction away from their approach course. The ship seemed to be avoiding a collision but was still circling wide of their position.

Oh, great and blessed Ra, holy ruler of the Two Horizons, of earth, sky and the underworld, the ancient deceiver has seen us, and his captain means to ram us. What shall we do?

They all heard the directed thoughts of one of the pirates and became instantly focused on him. Mirrortac forgot about the heaving motions of the ship as he listened with the others to the one-sided telepathic conversation.

Oh, wise and holy Ra, your command shall be done!

Mitac frowned and pretended to be Ra. *And what is that command? Repeat it to me.*

Who speaks? Is this the ancient deceiver? The pirate queried.

You question the great and holy Ra? Mitac said.

You are the deceiver! You are not Ra.

It is true. I am not Ra ... but it is he who deceives.

Prepare for your death, demon! ... Holy Ra, the ancient deceiver speaks to me and accuses you.

Ameece and the erfins heard no more but all felt a darkness of mood descend upon them. The boat slowed. They could hear a commotion issuing from the ship's bridge and turned to see the captain struggling with Kelly. The captain was trying to open the door to the outside gangway, but Kelly was preventing him. Then the man slumped into the Ancient's arms. Kelly laid him down and called out to the crew, but the men ran over to the sides and jumped off into the sea. Kelly swore and cut the engine, leaving the boat drifting to a halt as the other vessel turned towards them.

Kelly dashed down from the wheelhouse and across to where the five stood gaping at the water where the crew were drowning.

'I had to subdue the captain, but I couldn't get all the crew. Ra used the pirates' crystals to put a hex on the men and make them end it. He must not want us dead yet or you'd be down there with Davey Jones as well,' Kelly said.

'Which one is Davey Jones?' Treetam asked.

Kelly flashed a smile. 'That's just a name for the sea.'

Mirrortac sighed. 'What do we do now? These pie-rats will take us.'

Kelly patted the erfin on the shoulder. 'I think it will be all right. Just trust me.'

The erfin scrunched up his face at him and Mitac gave him a cheeky smile.

'Love your confidence big mate,' he mocked.

'Wish I had my bow right now,' Ezof added.

Kelly chuckled before all their attention was drawn to the vessel sidling up to their boat. Men wearing loose clothing and head coverings appeared on deck with rifles in their hands. They aimed their guns into the air and shot off a round before casting ropes over and jumping onto the deck where Kelly and the five watched motionless. They tied off the two ships together and one man wearing a white scarf around his head stepped ahead of the others. He swaggered towards them, his rifle slung with a strap around one shoulder and chains of bullets wrapped around his chest.

The man pointed his rifle at them and menaced them with it. 'You come with us!' he said.

Ezof growled and was about to rush him when Kelly forestalled him.

'You don't want to be doing that, little mate. Those things they are carrying not only make a lot of noise, but they can kill you in a flash.'

'Yeah, little mate!' the gunman mocked, and waved his gun at the young erfin. 'We don't want no holes in you. The most sacred one prefers you in one piece ... but he won't mind if we have to shoot off a few of your toes.'

Ezof backed off but grunted and bared his teeth.

The other men moved in and jabbed the erfins with their guns.

'On the boat!' the leader commanded.

'What do you want with us?' Treetam asked.

'You don't ask no questions!'

The head man nodded at one of the men who pushed her roughly towards the other boat.

Treetam glared back at him but complied.

Seeing this, Ezof turned and bit the man hard on the arm. The man swore and immediately whacked Ezof in the head with the rifle butt. The shorter erfin swung around again and tackled the man with such force that the two sprawled to the ground. Other men rushed in and manhandled the erfin, striking him and kicking him until he finally relented. Two men then grabbed him and dragged him towards the side of the ship.

Treetam winced as she saw how Ezof was being handled and noted his bruised face and the blood trickling down from a wound on the back of his head. Despite this, Ezof still snarled and struggled against his captors as they forced him onto the adjacent deck.

Mirrortac and Ameece looked on in shock as Mitac boarded the other boat. Kelly peered at the scene in silent sympathy while waiting for all to board the pirates' vessel.

The head man instructed one of his men to search the dhow for any other survivors, and after a few minutes they all heard a loud bang before the man returned and muttered something to the leader, then joined the others.

Kelly sighed and glanced at the erfins with a look that they all understood – the captain was dead.

The leader, Khadar, was a swarthy man who had dark brown eyes with pale yellow whites. He had his men tie the captives' hands behind their backs and marched them into a cabin where three of his men guarded them with their rifles.

Mirrortac placed his hand on Ezof's head and began to meditate, and as he did so, his hand warmed, and the wound started to heal. The others had witnessed Mirrortac's healing ability before, but Kelly raised an eyebrow.

'We Ancients never taught you that, my friend. You certainly are full of surprises,' he said.

The three pirates shook their heads and one said, 'He is a witch doctor. I have heard of them in our villages.'

Mirrortac stared back at the men and returned an enigmatic smile but said nothing.

Days passed as the dhow sailed towards the coast of Somalia. They ate raw fish and a flatbread that reminded Mirrortac of the bread he ate back in his homeland Eol. They soon realised that their foe was taking them exactly where they wanted to go to retrieve the stone, albeit under an armed guard who had no manners. The Somalians would be handing them over to others in Somalia who were to take them to Egypt. Kelly surmised that they would not be taken along the faster route of the Red Sea, which would give Ra time to fully take control and avoid any attempt at retrieving the Einuk stone before the triad of the planets was established.

It was night when they were taken ashore, and Kelly was acting agitated. He kept staring up into the sky and muttering under his breath. Mitac was curious and looked up too as they were being marched up a sandy beach towards a group of shadowy figures standing on the opposite foreshore. A sprinkling of stars spread across the sky, fixed in their slow progress through the heavens. But soon Mitac noticed that several stars were visibly moving.

'Wa-ku has brought his people to help us,' he remarked.

Kelly frowned. 'I don't think these have come to help you. Just call it a gut feeling.'

The others were now looking up too, but their captors were pushing them along.

'You are sick in gut? Argh, it is just the food you ate.' Mitac said.

'What would make you say this?' Ameece inquired of Kelly, staring up at the moving dots and trying not to trip.

'There has been no communication with me. I would know if it was your friend Wa-ku.'

'Perhaps they do not wish Ra to know they are here,' Mitac ventured.

'Hope I'm wrong, little mate. But I never am about these feelings. I am an Ancient, remember.'

The shadows at the end of the beach started to take form. They were stubby and short, and looked suspiciously like erfins. Mirrortac's hackles prickled as they neared the waiting group. One of the figures raised a fat palm to call them to a stop, and the pirates halted and backed away.

'You! Come here to us,' he said in erfinish.

The men had already turned and left, while the erfins along with Ameece and Kelly moved forward.

A group of ten burly erfins took form. They were warriors in the battle dress of wolf hide belts with metal breastplates inscribed with the head of a nite-wolf. Their fur was thick and grey, and they carried ancient swords engraved with sacred maja symbols.

The triplets all stared at the erfins with confused expressions.

Ameece voiced what they were all thinking. 'You are all erfins. Where did you come from? How did you get here?'

The erfin who had raised his hand now spoke. 'Is that what you say we are? We are in the service of the great Ra, and it be our duty to take you to him.'

'Do you naught remember?' Ameece queried.

'We have slept for many moons. We remember nothing of our past; only that Ra is our god and that our duty be to him.'

'Ra has bewitched you,' Mirrortac scowled.

'Do not insult the name of your god, or I will smite you with my sword!' the erfin growled.

Ameece turned to Mirrortac. 'Where could these have come from?'

Mirrortac pondered before answering. 'Do you recall the discernment we had when in Yidrogh? It was my life as Merftac the warrior.'

Ameece mused for a few moments then brightened. 'Yes! You fought a battle then went into the giant forest ... the one where our triplets were born.'

'Do you recall the cosmo-ship taking many of the warriors with it?'

She nodded then stared at the warrior erfins. 'These must be those warriors ... but ... how is it that they live now, so many many moons later?'

'Ra must have put them into a deep sleep and used his magic to bring them back to life.'

The triplets gaped at the ancient erfins. Ezof was especially impressed.

'Holy sons of Yu!' he cried. 'Were you a warrior like these in your last life, dada,' he asked.

'Indeed, I was Merftac who led these same ones.'

The warriors stirred at the sound of the name and frowned when none of them could place where they knew it.

'You know it, don't you?' Mitac said, addressing the warriors.

The erfins turned to each other murmuring.

'You know him – Merftac – the great warrior who led you in Eol! He is here with us as Mirrortac,' Mitac emphasised, attempting to trigger their memories.

There were more murmurs among them as they exchanged conflicted glances.

'This trickery will naught change our duty,' the leader said. 'We will take you to Ra when he be ready. You come with us now.'

'By what name are you called?' Mirrortac queried of the leader.

'The great Ra has given me the name RaBast.'

'But what of your true name?'

'This be my true name as Ra decrees. We be all reborn to serve the holy one above all holy ones.'

'Then let us go to Ra, RaBast,' Mirrortac said.

The warrior nodded. 'We rest until dawn. We have our tents a short footfall from here.'

The captives were led inland about 500 metres to a collection of ragged tents just high enough for an erfin to stand in and as wide as three metres. Laying on the ground nearby were ten large creatures with humps on their backs and smelling of dust and unwashed hair. The triplets were all put into one tent with three of the warriors; Mirrortac and Ameece together with another three in the second tent, while

Kelly had to sleep with four warriors around him in the third tent.

There was only a glimmer of light in the east when they were all roused, and the tents collapsed and rolled up. A faint warm breeze rustled their cloaks as all the captives were given loose robes to wear and hoisted onto the animals with the tents, supplies and warrior riders.

The journey west was slow and lumbering, taxing Mirrortac's rheumatic leg and rubbing against the captives' thighs and buttocks. The breeze quickly dissipated into a constant dry heat despite the sun having not yet risen. The landscape was arid with only irregular grass tussocks and an occasional tree struggling up from the ground. Townships became few and far between, with little sign of people, and those who they saw were mostly dark skinned tending small herds of the horned bovine creatures that Kelly identified as cattle. When the sun peeked up above the horizon, the temperature rose swiftly to a stifling level, reminding Mirrortac of the Wastes of Nug that he crossed after living with the faugs in the forest.

The creature camels carried their weight with little complaint, displaying a strong stamina that kept them moving across the hundreds of kilometres of harsh dry land. Sometimes they stopped at water wells to replenish the supply for the caravan and allow the camels to graze on the plant growth available. They set up camp each night and left well before sunrise to take advantage of the cooler conditions while they could.

After several days' travel, the landscape began to transition into hilly country littered with boulders and rocks that tested the camels' footing. The erfin warriors avoided the larger towns and cities, skirting the ranges away from prying eyes and major routes.

The captives grew weary as the days slipped past, with progress far too slow. 'We must find a vehicle and be done with these creatures,' Mirrortac remarked to Kelly. 'Can you naught put these erfins to sleep so we may make our escape?'

'Normally mate, I could, but the crystals put them under Ra's total control,' Kelly explained. 'But I'm working on an idea ...'

'You must work harder, we are running out of time,' Mirrortac said.

Kelly gave the erfin an appraising glance. 'Perhaps you can help me with an idea of your own, since you were chosen for this mission. You might not like what I come up with.'

'I am too aware of being this chosen one ... but now in a world of men I cannot see what an erfin and his kin can do.'

Mitac, who had been listening, hastened his camel to come alongside them. 'These erfins know you, dada ... they just don't remember. You must ask to see RaBast's sword,' he said.

'And he will just give it to me I'm sure,' Mirrortac grunted.

'I believe he will when we explain that all the other nine are armed against you; no contest!'

'He's got a point,' Kelly said. 'It's a crazy idea, but then ...'

Hours later they stopped at a well where they allowed the camels and themselves some time to drink and eat. Mitac nodded at Mirrortac who begrudgingly approached RaBast and asked to see his sword.

'You wish to kill me with it?' he said.

'No. How can it be that I could kill you when you have all your warriors armed and ready to take me. I merely wish to admire this old weapon of my people.'

RaBast motioned to his warriors to surround the erfin should he try anything nasty, then unsheathed his sword before presenting it into Mirrortac's hands.

The elder erfin held it with reverence as he beheld its jewel encrusted hilt and the fine edge of the sword, and the raw symbol on its hilt of a wolf in full attack. Immediately, he was transported back to the time of Merftac. He felt the weight of the armour and the cry of his fellow warriors as they battled the mountain dwelling Madin. He smelled the rich scent of earth and green things as he and his warriors wandered the Faug Forest. He saw the cosmo-ship land and the god-like men lead a chosen number of his warriors to the ship. He saw him hand this sword to his trusted friend before he and 49 others were taken away into the Greater Sky. He mouthed his friend's name as the sword changed hands – *Caafritac.*

'Caafritac,' he murmured.

He raised his eyes up to RaBast who was staring back at the elder erfin with a look of consternation before again regaining his composure.

'My sword?' RaBast extended his arms to take the sword back.

'My sword? Merftac's sword,' Mirrortac said. 'Your real name is Caafritac.'

The warrior gestured with his hands to take his sword back. 'What name I may have been known by before is of no consequence. I belong to Ra now ... great and holy Ra!' he shouted.

The warrior trembled as his eyes teared up. 'My sword!'

Mirrortac surrendered the sword, and with it Merftac's memories. He felt suddenly exhausted and had to sit down.

RaBast abruptly turned his back to them and sheathed his sword as he walked away.

Kelly looked at Mirrortac and Mitac with a glint of pride. 'Whoever chose you, chose well. You guys are no mere erfins.'

However, RaBast soon had them back on the camels as though nothing had transpired and was directing them towards the north across rugged country.

Ameece tried to console her erfin. 'You tried,' she said, wrapping her arms around him from behind on the camel they shared.

'Yep, for a moment there I thought you had him,' Kelly remarked from behind. 'Don't feel bad, little buddy; Ra's crystals are potent stuff. He's got a good hold on them.'

Right then they heard a roar in the sky before a squadron of jets thundered over their heads towards the north. All the erfins covered their ears and cowered down on their animals at the sudden noise and sight of the war machines. They had barely recovered from the fright when another squadron followed, then another and another. The air and ground shook with the noise like a dragon in full fury.

'Not everyone has sided with Ra,' Kelly said. 'These refuse to wear the crystals and will make war with him.'

The captives and the erfin warriors all looked up and wondered about the purpose of all these jets.

'Way to go! Do they carry blazing arrows?' Ezof cried out.

'Something like that ... missiles that can blow up buildings into pieces,' Kelly said.

'Like the solar-bites,' Treetam said, swinging her head around from the camel in front.

'Yes, like them but much more primitive,' Kelly said. 'But the effect is the same ... just as destructive.'

'Then they will make this Ra blow up,' Ezof cried, punching the air with his fist.

Kelly shook his head. 'Ra is more powerful than you realise.'

He had no sooner said that when there was a swooshing sound and a vibration in the air. Suddenly, it seemed a legion of stars were falling to earth, but as they descended, the watchers caught a glint of metal and the now familiar appearance of many cosmo-ships speeding towards them at a rate far greater than the jets that came before. The ships levelled off a short distance above the ground and shot northwards on the same track as the jets. Their speed was such that the few trees struggling up from between the rocky ground were snapped in half by the force of the wind generated, and a whirlwind of dust and debris swirled up beneath them into the distance.

Kelly cursed out loud and swept his hands to his head as though experiencing a headache.

Ezof punched the air again and hooted with glee. 'Ra will get it now!'

Kelly looked at him without saying a word, his face pallid and drawn.

'What?' the young erfin said. 'Be this not your kin gone to take Ra?'

'Are you not listening?' Kelly remarked with a pained look.

Ezof was about to say something then went quiet.

Enemy is in sight. Shall we eliminate, Lord Ra?

Ezof swallowed hard while the others dropped their heads in dismay.

Eliminate as you see fit, came Ra's reply, now clearly heard in their minds for the first time.

The thundering roar of an approaching jet came in from the north before they saw it closely dogged by one of the cosmo-ships. The jet was trying to escape but it was no match for the speed of the cosmo-ship. A sharp flash came out from it and struck the jet, and immediately it burst into dark smoke and flame, and flipped through the air until it hit the ground with an explosion that rocked the earth all around. An acrid smell of aviation fuel and rubber and flesh drifted across the party who gaped in stunned silence at the scene of destruction. Even the warriors stopped their camels to stare in disbelief.

'Hail the greatness and power of Ra!' one of them shouted.

'All hail Ra!' the others cried.

'I do not understand,' Mirrortac said, staring at the wreckage. 'Are these not your kin?' He turned to Kelly.

'I haven't quite got the whole story either,' Kelly shrugged. 'But Ra has some mates among our people.'

'Obvo,' Treetam remarked, and despite the mood, Kelly had to smile back at her.

'Where did you get that expression,' he said.

Treetam simply shrugged. 'I hear the Nerthulian youth's speech in my mind.'

Another sharp flash erupted in the distance followed by an explosion and billowing dark clouds of smoke. The distant explosions continued throughout the day as they made their way slowly north-west. The landscape became more mountainous as they wound through gorges and negotiated around boulders and over stony ground. Trees and scrub were scattered here and there punctuated by bold outcrops of rock that rose barren and stark. The camels found pastures to graze and restore their strength, while village farms fed the party. Villagers remained out of sight in their huts, peering out fearfully at the furry aliens. The erfin warriors slaughtered goats for their meat and helped themselves to village crops without regard.

After several days, they reached an area of streams and waterfalls. Groups of various animals were evident, and monkeys chattered in the trees. Kelly seemed unusually contemplative while everyone sensed something, or someone was watching them. The camels strode warily, snorting and fidgeting. Finally, the animals would go no further, and as soon as everyone had dismounted, they bolted away into the scrub carrying all their supplies.

'Now what?' Treetam exclaimed. 'We are stuck here.'

Kelly looked back and winked. 'My plan is about to come into play. Be ready to make our escape.'

The warrior erfins growled and drew their swords, glancing around with heightened alertness at the surrounding thickets. Kelly gestured for the party to remain close while also watching and listening for the ominous threat. They could hear nothing but the sighing of a breeze rustling the leaves, and glimpses of spotted patterns moving among the trees. The warriors' muscles flexed as they wielded their ancient swords, prepared for whatever might attack.

A guttural purr rose from various points around them before a blur of brown and orange erupted from the treeline and lunged at the warriors, ignoring the captives completely. Several large cats fell upon the warriors who collapsed under the weight of the animals. The leopards were strong and quickly wrapped their jaws around the warriors' thick necks and abdomens and were sinking their sharp incisors into the fur and flesh. The warriors were strong and fought back, pushing the cats off them and slicing at them with their swords.

'Come on ... this is our chance. Go!' Kelly yelled, and started to run towards a rocky outcrop nearby.

The captives froze at the sight before regaining their senses and fleeing, except Mirrortac who wanted to go to the aid of the warriors who had their hands full repelling the leopards.

'Don't worry about them! We have to go now,' Kelly shouted back at the erfin.

One of the cats was dead but the others were still making a mess of the warriors, opening gouging flesh wounds that gushed blood everywhere, weakening them. The leader stared back at Mirrortac with appealing eyes.

'Merftac ... I am sorry master. Leave us.'

The warrior collapsed as a leopard severed his jugular.

Mirrortac stood watching, his face stained with tears. He turned and joined the others as they disappeared behind the outcrop.

They were running towards a large pool and a waterfall.

'Prepare to get wet. We're taking a shortcut,' Kelly said, as he waded into the water and made straight for the curtain of water plunging down from above.

'Oops, wet ... no like,' Ezof said, cringing as he entered the water.

Treetam and Mitac also baulked at the cold water but continued behind Kelly and Ezof. Mirrortac shivered a little as he entered the water, holding Ameece's hand tight. They could only see Kelly's head above the water as he swam onward, and all of them struggled as their feet left the bottom. Mirrortac remembered his first swimming experience with the Meretees island people and helped Ameece keep her head up and breathing. The triplets were almost drowning as they sunk below the surface a few times before finding the bottom again nearer the waterfall, relieved they could again walk on the smooth stony stream bed.

Kelly disappeared through the waterfall which they all soon discovered hid a cavern soaked with moss and slimy algae. The interior revealed a sinuous passage into a subterranean maze that Kelly negotiated with confidence.

'What was that with the cats? Was that your plan?' Mitac asked Kelly.

'Yeah little mate. Leopards don't normally hunt like that, but as an Ancient I can manipulate their instincts to hunt a specific target. Neat hey?'

'You mean you can mind talk to them?' Treetam said.

'I guess that's a fair judgement. I had to guide them for days and distract the other prey so they'd be hungry enough to take on the warriors.'

'You mean scare off the other animals they eat?' Mitac said.

Kelly nodded then groped ahead in the darkness as they encountered a cavern dimly lit by glowworms.

'This is it. We're nearly there.'

'Where is there?' Mirrortac queried. 'Another portal?'

Kelly took out his lighter as he had in the other cave and lit a series of torches on the walls around them. The lustre of the Alexandrite glinted back at them in rainbow hues in a circle of crystal clusters. The Australian shoved his hand into a hollow in the nearby wall and recovered the crystal inserts that he needed to activate the portal. He slapped away a cockroach that had crawled onto his arm before striding over to the portal and placing the crystals.

Kelly muttered the activation code in a long string of indecipherable terms, then inserted the final crystal at the top of the circle. There was the familiar flash as the centre of the circle pulsed into glossy inkiness.

'Right, you know the drill; get through as quick as possible.'

'You killed my kin,' Mirrortac moaned.

The elder erfin looked at the man with an accusing eye.

'We'll discuss this later. Go quickly now!' Kelly urged.

'They were ready to let us go. He knew me ...' Mirrortac stubbornly stood his ground.

The Australian sighed. 'They were dead anyway. It's all for the best ... for the greater good.'

'Such a terrible death.' Mirrortac shook his shaggy head.

'I am sorry. We could not know if they would let us go in time. The lives of so many depend on us retrieving Einuk. Now go!'

Ezof led the way with Kelly passing through last. A clap of his hands and the portal collapsed behind them. It was pitch dark and musty, but the wall felt regular whenever someone stumbled up against it. Kelly thumbed his lighter and lit a single torch perched on the wall near the portal. A sputtering flame revealed a chamber with stone walls engraved with figures and hieroglyphs. Figures of people were attending others with the head of a falcon and jackal and standing on large canoes.

'Who are these?' asked Mitac. 'Are we inside a dwelling?'

'Ancient Egyptians,' Kelly said. 'We're inside a pyramid ... deep inside. Nobody in the modern world knows of this section.'

'Pyramid?' they said together.

'A pyramid has a triangle shape, like this.' Kelly made the shape with his hands. 'It's a place where the Egyptian people used to bury their pharaohs, the royalty, as good as gods as far as they were concerned. They'd anoint the bodies in fragrant oils and wrap them in cloth to prepare them for the journey to the underworld.'

Treetam crimped her nose. 'Ew, so there are dead people in here?'

'That there are, but not in this section. This was especially made for us Ancients to come and go as we pleased.'

'They knew of you?' Ameece appeared surprised.

'Indeed, they did ... but the modern Egyptians no longer know of us. We once were part of the guidance to build the pyramids. Burying pharaohs was just a cover. The whole purpose was to set up a cosmic network ... well, until Ra came along and stuffed it all up for the rest of us.'

'So, we are in a building for the dead that is not a building for the dead but a portal of sorts?' Mitac queried.

'It be no normal building,' Mirrortac volunteered. 'It be like a mountain of rock with a point at the top.'

'How do you know of this?' Treetam asked. 'You have not been on Nerthule before.'

Mirrortac massaged his beard. 'The pyramid I saw was on Mareos ... on Plumer-Ra ... the main island of the Meretees. It was joined once to Nerthule, but no more.'

'Hmmm, interesting,' Kelly remarked. 'You say it was on an island the people called Plumer-Ra?'

The elder erfin inclined his head in agreement.

'And were there any other uses of the word 'Ra' on that island?'

Mirrortac nodded. 'Yeah. The keepers of the pyramid were called Ra-finelles and they met in the Chamber of Ra ... Ra's name was everywhere in the pyramid.'

'Ra must've set up that pyramid before heading here,' Kelly said. 'He will have a pyramid hidden in the desert somewheres in Egypt ... although not so hidden anymore. We have to find it and get in somehow to retrieve the Einuk stone.'

'That will be simpleness,' Mirrortac said with sarcasm.

'We might be inside Ra's pyramid now,' Ezof said with an edge of hope.

Kelly shook his head. 'If only it was that easy, little mate. Ra's pyramid is a metal and crystalline structure. This one's just a much smaller stone version.'

The Ancient glanced around the stone walls of the chamber.

'But first thing's first; we must find a way out of here,' he said.

Everyone's attention was drawn to the walls and the lack of any visible exit. Except for where they had entered, all the walls were solid without any door evident.

'It's been maybe a thousand years since I've been through here, and the

Egyptians have since shut off this chamber and forgotten about it. I'm betting though, that there's a mechanism to open it from this side.'

'And if there's not?' Mitac asked.

'Then we go to Plan B ... which means going back through the portal and traipsing hundreds of clicks to get here.'

The others gave him puzzled looks and scratched their heads. Kelly ignored them and started examining the walls and the pictograms. 'Aha!' he said, then pushed his fingers against some of the icons which immediately depressed into the wall. There was a sudden inrush of air at the same time as a large block of stone detached from the wall, leaving an opening large enough for a person to slide through to the other side.

'Okay, let's go.' He gestured for them to follow.

They each passed through the gap and into a dark hallway. Kelly thumbed his lighter and led the way to a series of steps and passages. Like the chamber, the walls of the hall and passages were adorned in a rich tapestry of Egyptian life. Scorpions and beetles scurried out of their way while the passages echoed to the sound of their breathing. An occasional snake would slither through cracks in the wall but avoided the shadows looming up at them along the passages. At last they reached what appeared to be a dead end in a twin chamber. Kelly walked to an alcove between the two chambers and shuffled his feet over the dusty floor to reveal a star composed of two equilateral triangles that created six points.

'I want you all to stand with me here. Make sure you are all standing over the star on the floor,' Kelly instructed.

They all huddled up with Kelly over the star shape before he started muttering and stamping on the floor. Within seconds the floor started to rise, and the portion of ceiling above lifted through with much grinding. They were gradually elevated into another chamber above them until the star form was level with the floor of the new chamber. Kelly ushered them into the chamber before again muttering his incantation that sent the star and ceiling portion descending back into the lower chamber until there was no evidence of the star shape or the twin chamber.

'We are in the known part of the pyramid now,' he said. 'We can make our way out through the passage ahead.'

The group followed Kelly through a level passage and past a side passage that had been chained off and lit as though with portions of sunlight. The hieroglyphs and visual representations of Egyptians and their lifestyles of thousands of years before had been restored to a vivid clarity. Here were statues and reliefs executed in fine detail. The main passage led them down and then up a narrow stairway with a timber railing for assisting people to make the steep ascent. Finally, they emerged on the outside and could look up at the triangular shape of the pyramid and its construction of stone blocks. The entrance was squared off with large stone pillars, and more pyramids punctuated the desert nearby.

A pungent odour of jet fuel and burning rubber drifted across the sands, and as they all looked out to the desert, they could see black smoke rising in many places, and nearby the remnants of fighter planes still smouldering.

'We've got to look for a truck to get us closer to Ra's pyramid, and that will be no easy task.' Kelly started to take big steps from the pyramids to a road on the other side.

'We could do with some solar-bites right now,' Ezof growled.

Treetam nodded. 'Could be right there, bro,' she said.

Mitac halted and frowned. 'What is martial law?' he asked.

'What did you say?' Kelly stopped and faced the erfin.

'Martial law? I heard the voice in my mind; someone calling himself President Mustafa El Amman.'

'Yes, I heard it too,' Treetam confirmed.

Kelly frowned. 'It means that this country is under the control of the armed forces ... soldiers and military people. It also means that we cannot roam around freely without the permission of the army.'

'But if we are in the cloth of the soldier?' Mitac mused.

'Yes, that may work; but then we'll have to steal some uniforms, and even with uniforms you guys will stick out like the proverbial sore thumb. You are the enemy now.'

'My thumb is not sore, but my legs are,' Mirrortac pointed out.

'We'll hide you all in the back of an army truck. Wait here and don't attract any attention.'

Kelly ran off towards the road and later returned driving an armoured personnel carrier (APC) with high clearance from the ground. He emerged dressed in an Egyptian army uniform and was grinning from ear to ear.

'You may call me Captain Kelly,' he jested.

'How ...?'

'A little charm and persuasion, but you don't need to know the details,' he said, clipping off Ezof's question. 'All you need to do is get in the back out of sight.'

Mirrortac noticed the Australian's cheek was bruised and reached out and brushed his hand against the man's cheek as he passed to get into the vehicle.

Kelly smiled. 'Thanks, Mirrortac, I needed that. It was all in the line of duty, you know.'

'I'm sure it was,' Treetam said and patted him on the other cheek while giving him a wry smile.

* * *

They joined a convoy of APCs and other military vehicles progressing towards the west of Cairo towards Ra's pyramid. Wreckage of planes and ground attack vehicles littered the desert while cosmo-ships patrolled the corridor leading up to the pyramid still some distance away. Hostilities had halted against Ra and his forces after the loss of many lives. The convoy retrieved bodies along the way while Mirrortac's group listened in to the minds of the leaders of Egypt, Israel, the USA, Europe and the surrounding Middle Eastern Arab states who had all gathered in Cairo to discuss the alien incursion. Pro-Ra sympathisers had been creating havoc in Europe and America, with the 'dark crystal brigade' as the media dubbed them, rioting in the streets of the major capitals and cities of what was called the 'free world'. The leaders of some countries had also succumbed to the dark crystals craze and had sent their armies against anyone opposing the rule of Ra.

After a full day of travel, stopping often to pick up bodies of the dead, the convoy camped across from the battle front where hundreds of soldiers and vehicles had disintegrated into ash. It was the line surrounding the pyramid from where no-one could pass unless permitted. An electro-magnetic pulse field guarded the massive metal pyramid and destroyed anything attempting to enter. Tents and marquees were set up for generals and their staff to discuss battle strategies, but until they worked out a way to circumvent the pulse field, all was at a loss to conquer Ra's defences.

Ameece grabbed the communication stone hanging around her neck as it started to buzz and throb against her chest. When she looked, it was glowing a deep tangerine.

Ameece glanced back at Mirrortac and the stone. 'We are near Einuk, my one. Can you speak to Evarngar?'

Hail Mirrortac! You have the stone? came a voice in the elder erfin's head.

'It is Wa-ku; he speaks in my head,' Mirrortac said to the others.

Ameece and the triplets exclaimed together, 'We hear him too!'

Kelly gasped and stared back at them. 'Oh, my heavens! I feel the presence of another Ancient!'

JOURNEY ACROSS THE COSMOS

The *Petrichor* emerged from the Nerthulian portal like a piece of flotsom spat out of a storm drain. The planet was still tens of millions of kilometres away on the converse plane upon which the sun's solar system orbited. Cibell and Thar-karn hooted loudly like excited children.

'Another good one,' Thar-karn chuckled. His belly heaved with his infectious laughter.

Cibell twirled his long moustache while grinning his agreement.

Wa-ku and Hathor were still trying to focus their eyes as the ship slowed in its spinning and automatically aligned itself towards Nerthule which presented as a tiny white spot ahead.

Hathor clutched at her chest and looked towards Wa-ku. 'I can feel him ...' she said as her eyes swivelled back towards the combined two Stones of Destiny lying on the floor.

Oashu and Darm were glowing a bright golden red and making a soft crackling sound.

'Einuk is near?' Wa-ku stared wide-eyed at Hathor.

'He is near too,' she said. 'You can talk to him, them.'

'You mean Mirrortac is near?'

'Well yes,' she faulted. 'But the Ancient one of Nerthule is also near.'

He reached for the slot on the greenstone screen to activate the transmitter, but Hathor forestalled him with her hand.

'That is no use to you. The connection stone is telepathically operated,' she said.

His hand was still poised over the control when he said, 'Oh ... I am not used to that.'

'Give it a try, love,' she said, and the dimples on her cheeks crimped with mirth.

Wa-ku let his hand drop. 'Oh ... kay.'

Hathor grabbed his hand and placed it on the conjoined Stones of Destiny.

All of a sudden, he *felt* several minds.

Hail Mirrortac! You have the stone? he communicated.

There was a feeling of excitement emanating from the minds of the erfins.

Nay! Einuk is in the hands of the one called Ra. He has a great shining pyramid and is in command of Nerthule, Mirrortac said.

Who is the Ancient with you? came another voice.

Ahh ...

Just call me Hathor for now, she interjected.

My human name is Kelly; James Kelly, he said.

She sensed his amusement in the tone of his communication.

I always wanted to say that ... the Nerthulians have a legendary hero they made up called James Bond. He's a bit of an ass-kicker of bad guys, Kelly said.

Hathor's face lit up. *I see, Mister Kelly. And will you be kicking Ra's 'ass' as you say?*

We certainly hope so, came the answer. *Which reminds me ... do you have the other two stones?*

Yes. They are fully activated and linked in with Einuk.

Good. We're going to need them to get us ...

Stop! Ra is listening! Hathor warned.

Oh shit! Kelly said. *There's another problem too.*

I know, Mister Kelly. I know what it is. We will work something out this end.

Hathor pulled Wa-ku's hands off the stones and immediately cupped her own palms above them. Her eyes flipped up, revealing their whites as she fell into a self-induced trance. She started muttering loudly in the secret language of maja until the glow of the stones extinguished. Then she got up and looked straight at Wa-ku.

'We can expect company at any moment. The men will be busy,' she said, gesturing towards Cibell and Thar-karn.

Wa-ku's face turned a few shades lighter. 'You heard her, boys. Get the guns ready.'

Nerthule had turned from a white spot into a blue orb floating in space, with its moon also visible.

They watched as several objects rose from the planet and rapidly approached in their direction.

'Argh, my shoulder hurts already. I hate war,' Wa-ku moaned.

'I don't much like it either,' Hathor said.

Wa-ku switched on the greenstone screen. 'Squadron Leader Zenon, requesting urgent assistance. This is the *Petrichor*. We will soon be under attack.'

The speaker fizzled before a male voice answered. 'Got you *Petrichor*. We have your position marked. We were awaiting your arrival.'

A fleet of enemy cosmo-ships came into view as Cibell and Thar-karn swung their plasma guns towards them.

There was a shudder as the plasma guns were fired in unison. The cosmo-ships evaded them and spread out around them. Several bright flashes erupted from the enemy ships' guns. Wa-ku flung the ship at an angle as the magnesium bright rays shot past perilously close. He banked steeply, flinging them tightly against their seat restraints.

Wa-ku swore. Cibell cursed.

'Come here you three-eyed twit!' Thar-karn shouted, firing off another round of plasma shots.

The side of an enemy ship took a hit, sending debris twirling into space. Wa-ku kept busy eluding the plasma rays that came at the *Petrichor* from every angle.

'Come on squadron! We're in trouble here!'

A fleet of friendly ships appeared from behind the Moon and immediately engaged the enemy. Wa-ku escaped to the side of the fray while ships on both sides took damage. He accelerated towards Mars.

'Where's an asteroid when you need one?' he muttered.

An enemy ship broke off from the battle and pursued them.

'Damn!' Wa-ku cried, watching the monitor.

The pursuit ship rapidly gained on the *Petrichor*.

'It's a superior make. They had plenty of time to build their warships. It's been a long time planning.'

Hathor stood and massaged his shoulders in silence. Beads of sweat ran down his forehead as he manoeuvred the *Petrichor* to shake off the pursuit ship.

Cibell and Thar-karn swivelled their guns and fired several times. A blast from the other ship thundered into the side thrusters, flipping the *Petrichor* into a spin.

'The port side thruster is out, sir,' Thar-karn shouted.

Wa-ku regained control in time for Cibell to score a minor hit to the enemy ship.

'Yes! Take that you slimy galactic worm!' he shouted.

'Reverse flip and fire!' Hathor shouted suddenly.

Wa-ku reacted without question, pulling the ship into a steep ascending turn, and firing the retro-blasters. The metal screeched as the ship went into a tight reverse manoeuvre that placed it directly facing the enemy cosmo-ship.

Both Cibell and Thar-karn immediately locked on and fired.

The enemy ship splintered into a million pieces that exploded in all directions. A tresoculi body thunked against the front screen of the *Petrichor* and disintegrated into dust. Large chunks of metal clattered against the ship's exterior, making a noisy racket as the exploded pieces sprayed the ship.

'There's an asteroid at Nav. 0000562X from us, sir,' Cibell said.

Wa-ku gave him the okay sign and logged in the navigation point.

'There's a flat area where we can land, then you Cibell can go out and see whether the port thruster can be repaired,' Wa-ku said.

Cibell gave a casual salute and got up to put on his suit.

Thar-karn also disengaged himself from the gunner seat and shook his blond curls.

'I could go a stiff brew right now,' he said, wiping sweat off his forehead.

'A nice cold one,' Cibell called from across the deck.

As soon as the ship landed, Wa-ku turned to Hathor and surprised her with a kiss.

Her eyes lit up and a cheeky smile appeared. 'Hmm, I could get used to that,' she said.

'That's for saving our lives,' he said.

'Oh ... anytime my blue-eyed superman.'

Cibell entered the airlock and shut the hatch. He was soon outside climbing over the *Petrichor* to the port thruster. Thar-karn manned the instruments to monitor Cibell's progress on the thruster.

The planet Nerthule and its moon were both shielded from view, as the *Petrichor* was on the far side of the asteroid.

##

Mitac looked back at Kelly. 'What just happened?'

Kelly massaged his chin and appeared worried. 'The other Stones of Destiny on the ship are linking with Einuk, and that means Ra knows where they are and will try to stop them.'

'Will he destroy the ship with the stones?' Mirrortac said.

'Yeah mate. But he can't destroy the stones; they'll just float in space for Ra's cronies to pick them up.'

'But the one named Hathor has broken the link,' Mitac mused.

'Hmm yeah, but it may not have been in time, and now we have no idea of what the hell is going on up there.'

Mitac remained thoughtful for a few moments before lifting his face to Kelly. 'It may be that we *can* know. We do not need the stones to "talk" to them.'

'How do you mean?' Kelly said.

The others turned to Mitac in expectation.

'The essence the faugs gave us allows us to talk mind to mind or to enter into the thoughts of others.'

Ezof and Treetam were so delighted with Mitac's revelation that they hugged and nuzzled him.

'Way to go bro!' Ezof cried.

'Now why didn't I think of that,' Treetam said.

Ameece nuzzled him. 'That is my youngling!'

Mirrortac smiled at Kelly who was grinning back at him.

'Brilliant mate! So, let's do this. Can you let me in on the convo, guys?'

There was no answer, but all of them concentrated on the communication with Hathor and Wa-ku. Minds combined and searched the field of mind voices to find the ones they wanted. It was no easy task as the minds of the world were like a clamouring crowd.

* * *

Hathor! Hathor!

'What?' Hathor rubbed at her forehead.

'Are you talking to me, love?' Wa-ku said, turning his head from the monitor.

'No. I thought someone was calling my name. That's odd.'

Hathor! Wa-ku!

'Yes?' they replied in unison then peered quizzically at each other.

'You heard that too, my dear?'

Hathor and Wa-ku. It's us ... Mitac and the others.

'Oh dear, they are using telepathy without the stones!' Hathor said in an excited voice. 'What clever little beings these friends of yours are.'

Aren't they just. Now we can all join in ... er ... this is Kelly, he said.

Wonderful, Mister Kelly. I am just becoming used to being an Ancient. I am just a nurse, really, or was ... this is so much, Hathor blurted.

Oh ... an Ancient is co-habiting with you; most unusual. Something drastic must have happened on Kosmo. Do you know of an Ancient dying recently? Kelly said.

Why yes ... Maru. She was drugged and taken by the Black Brotherhood, then gave up her life to protect the Pool of Knowledge.

This is a lot worse than I expected, Kelly said. *Maru was the last living Ancient in Kosmo. And she's using you now to guard against this Black Brotherhood whoever they are.*

Hathor's expression changed as she took in an extended breath.

Yes, I am, came an aged woman's voice. *The brotherhood is comprised of the tresoculi who will stop at nothing to assume control over Nerthule. You have not been in the spirit for many generations, T'in-ka, ... only to change bodies, and now you are steeped in the ways of Nerthule and have forgotten much.*

I am at your service, oh holy Maru, Kelly said. *What must we do to end this? The three-eyes are already a strong force here on Earth and we are but few.*

I am also at your service, wise one, Mirrortac said. *This be a difficult mission for one such as I and my kin who walk with me.*

Beloved erfin, I have heard much of you, and am grateful for your service in freeing Mareos from Yidu ... but there is now a greater threat to Nerthule for which you are ill-equipped. And yet, it is in your destiny to play an important part in this.

And what be that? Ra has Einuk and soon will have total power over Nerthule, Mirrortac said.

Hathor could feel his frustration and anger. *You are not alone in this, erfin, nor are your children, your partner. I and T'in-ka are working with you ... and the duoculi forces. The solution is in your minds, and your minds are the solution.*

Why be it that such ones as you wise ones speak in riddles? came the frustrated reply.

The Ancient's tone echoed with mirth. *Yes, we are often accused of that. It is our way of drawing out the potential in the living ones.*

Wa-ku interjected. *Back-up forces are coming ... there are already some here, but they dare not attack until more have arrived.*

The Nerthulians are at the mercy of Ra and the three-eyes, Kelly said. *Their ships have destroyed many of the Nerthulian craft and Ra has placed a force field around the pyramid.*

We shall need to get the other stones to you ... they need to be earthed to provide you with a portal to Einuk, Maru said.

Kelly's sigh could be felt across the millions of kilometres that separated them. *Easier said than done, mate ... first you need to get close enough to beam them in without getting the crap shot out of you. And without Ra's cronies getting them off us.*

Leave that to us, T'in-ka. James Bond was a spy, was he not? And how do spies work? Maru posed.

He pretends ... Ahhh! Kelly cut off what he was going to say. *Say no more. Brilliant!*

Hathor came back to herself and smiled at Wa-ku. 'We have a tresoculi ship to capture,' she said to her astonished partner.

'I don't know about this. I'd rather stay on the sideline ...' Wa-ku screwed up his face.

'We'll get some help. We can leave the *Petrichor* here and take the stones with us,' she added.

Wa-ku turned to the greenstone communication screen. 'All right. I hope this will work,' he said, pressing a crystal into place to activate the screen.

The face of the force commander coalesced. 'What is your request, Wa-ku? We have orders to assist in any way possible,' Squadron Leader Zenon said.

'We need to come aboard with our payload. My gunners will guard the *Petrichor*.'

Wa-ku made no mention of their plan to capture an enemy ship in case they were listening in on their frequency.

'Understood. We will arrange pick-up. Send us your coordinates,' Zenon said.

Wa-ku keyed in the coordinates in the agreed code to avoid being found by anyone other than the duoculi forces.

'Well, it is done,' Wa-ku told Hathor.

She leaned up to him and kissed him softly.

'I don't like this as much as you, but I know it's the right thing to do. Maru gives me that assurance.'

She grabbed a large cloth and wrapped Darm and Oashu in it, then placed it on the transmission plate in preparation for the transfer. Wa-ku briefed the gunners on their duties during their absence, then all waited for the pick-up ship to arrive.

It was only minutes before the familiar form of the command ship appeared above the *Petrichor* and signalled its arrival. Wa-ku and Hathor gathered with the combined Stones of Destiny and soon found themselves aboard the other ship.

A bearded man approached Wa-ku and saluted. 'Welcome to *The Thor*.'

Wa-ku and Hathor bowed to the commander who wore a close-fitting white uniform.

'The pleasure is ours,' Wa-ku replied.

Zenon introduced them to his own crew of ten, including gunners, a nurse, navigator, strategist, and general stewards. They faced a vast array of screens and equipment that made the *Petrichor* pale in comparison. The command ship was easily four times the size and included several smaller excursion craft attached as well as three times the number of plasma guns.

'Now, what is the nature of your request that you should wish to come aboard?' Zenon asked.

Hathor spoke before Wa-ku could utter a word.

'We need to capture one of the enemy's ships intact so that we can go to the surface without detection,' she said.

Zenon looked somewhat surprised and massaged his beard in thought.

'No easy undertaking, woman. You speak boldly for a nurse.'

Wa-ku glided in front of her with his chair. 'She is no mere nurse. An Ancient inhabits her,' Wa-ku explained.

Hathor gave him an annoyed look. 'No "mere" nurse indeed. What would you do without us ... die, I should think,' she snapped.

Wa-ku tried to apologise but became flustered. 'I ... I ... simply meant ...'

Hathor pushed him aside and glared at Zenon. 'Yes, the Ancient Maru is with me. There will be an enemy ship in the outer region beyond the Moon in a few 20ths from now. It will be patrolling in search of the *Petrichor*. Board it and overcome its crew.'

Zenon bowed deeply. 'How can we board it, holy one? We don't know its transmission code.'

'I shall give you the code. You will need your four gunners and weapons. Leave us here until you have gained command.'

Wa-ku marvelled at the nurse who now spoke with authority and confidence. Zenon bowed again.

'As you command, holy one,' Zenon said, avoiding eye contact with the woman.

Zenon swung around and began to shout out commands to the gunners and the crew who swiftly mobilised. The gunners armed themselves with solar-bites and put on battle suits while the navigator directed the ship on a course towards the Moon. The general stewards went into the galley and soon emerged with food capsules to serve the guests.

Hathor blushed at her outburst as she withdrew alongside Wa-ku. He glanced at her and recognised those compassionate eyes that he fell in love with at the hospital.

'Welcome back, my love,' he said.

She smiled back coyly and hugged him.

'Maru can be tough,' she said. 'I think I like it.'

Wa-ku looked back with uncertainty but said nothing.

'Don't worry, dear. I will always be here,' she winked.

As predicted, it was only a few hours before they sighted the enemy patrol ship scouting past the Moon. Wa-ku knew that as they closed in to transmission range, the ship would spot them also and go into attack mode. They could not afford to waste a second; their boarding party would have to time it exactly before the tresoculi gunners started plasma blasting them. Hathor revealed the transmission code for the enemy which Zenon immediately keyed in before joining the gunners on the plate.

The navigator watched the distance reduce between the two ships as the enemy turned towards them. A flash erupted from it, forcing them to take evasive action. Zenon held his breath as he watched for the signal to activate the transmission beam. The enemy fired a second time, and the ship shuddered violently as they took a glancing blow.

The navigator nodded and pressed the transmission crystal into place.

Zenon and the gunners disappeared just as a third plasma beam shot out towards them. The navigator steered the ship away sharply, causing Hathor to lose her footing and fall to the floor. She stumbled up to her feet to grab hold of the nearest solid structure.

The enemy ship stopped firing but was swerving around in a haphazard way.

'We are winning,' Hathor said. 'But one of the gunners is injured.'

The drunken dance of the enemy ship ceased along with its deadly attitude towards them. The greenstone screen near the navigator burst into life as Zenon's image stared back at them.

'Squadron Leader Zenon reporting. We have captured the enemy ship and are in control ... of sorts,' he said.

Wa-ku moved over to the screen. 'Good job, sir. When can we come aboard?'

Zenon was short of breath. 'As soon as we have cleaned up here, Captain Wa-ku. You may need some instructing as to the ship's controls; they are quite different to what we are used to.'

Wa-ku rolled his eyes. 'Nothing is straight forward, but I am impressed that you have gained us the ship.'

Zenon paused before answering. 'One of my gunners is hurt. I will send him back first. He needs aid.'

'Go ahead, send the gunner.'

Zenon hesitated. 'You must beam him in from your side. As I said, the controls on this ship are quite different.'

Wa-ku glanced across to the navigator who nodded back his acknowledgment. He flicked a switch and soon a bloodied man appeared on the plate. There was a gash across his cheek, and one of his eyes was drooping towards it.

Hathor and the command ship nurse rushed to the man's aid and took him to the medical examination chamber. Wa-ku gagged and looked away. The sight of the torn flesh burned into his mind.

The stern-faced navigator eyed the captain with a touch of sympathy. 'You never really get used to it,' he said.

'Thanks,' Wa-ku said without enthusiasm.

One of the stewards offered him a biliousness pill but he waved him away.

It was quite some time before Hathor emerged from the medic chamber shaking her head.

'We stitched his face, but he's lost an eye,' she said.

'What happened? They wouldn't have been armed,' Wa-ku mused.

'One of the tresoculi threw him against a jagged component. It slashed his face open, but he kept fighting and overcame the brute,' she said.

'We need to get in there,' he said.

'Yes, they should be about ready for us now,' she said.

Wa-ku called up Zenon who was looking back with uncertainty.

'We don't know if you'll be able to operate this ship,' Zenon admitted. 'The tresoculi have created something altogether different; it's like nothing I've ever seen before.'

Hathor poked her head up in front of Wa-ku. 'We can handle it,' she told Zenon.

The squadron leader bowed. 'I do not doubt your word, holy one.'

Soon they both stood with the stones on the enemy ship's deck. Wa-ku gaped at the interior which was entirely comprised of angular crystal structures like one would expect to see in an underground cave. The only recognisable control was the one next to the only screen in the room – the communication terminal. The remainder of the ship was a forest of crystals and a maze of alleyways leading to other parts of the ship.

'I can't fly this thing!' he said with more than a hint of exasperation.

'Now you can see what I mean,' Zenon said. 'You can see for yourself, holy one; how can any of us fly this chemical concoction?'

Hathor gave a hint of a smile as she strolled over to one of the crystal structures. She stroked it with her palm, causing the ship to react with an accelerated movement towards the command ship.

'I shall fly it,' she said, lifting her head and eyeing the surprised faces around her.

Zenon bowed, and the other gunners followed his lead.

'Then can you send us back to our ship. I have to prepare for the battle ahead when the rest of the forces arrive.'

Hathor smiled and returned the bow. 'You may take the plate.'

'And we did manage to jettison the ... remains of the tresoculi crew into space, so you have the ship to yourselves,' Zenon said as he and the three gunners turned and walked onto the transmission plate.

Hathor bowed then reached up to a crystal above her head and stroked it. Before Wa-ku could say a word of farewell, the men had vanished.

##

The blue aura of Nerthule enveloped the planet in its glow as Hathor manoeuvred the ship towards a large brown patch on the surface. Wa-ku settled his hoverchair beside her as the cosmo-ship flew swiftly towards the planet. They were about to enter its atmosphere when the communication terminal burst into life.

'Alert! Alert! All outer rim ships must engage enemy in Moon quadrant 005. The duoculi have been hiding until back-up forces arrive.'

Hathor frowned. 'That means us.'

'We're almost in the inner rim. We must keep going,' Wa-ku said.

'Maybe they won't miss us,' she ventured.

A soft yellow glow surrounded the ship as they entered the stratosphere.

'Where are you going, *Isis Five*? You must engage enemy,' the speaker bellowed.

'That's our ship,' she said, sighing.

Wa-ku cursed out loud. 'We can't shoot at our own ships. Or risk being shot at!'

Hathor turned the ship around and shot back out towards the darkness of space. 'Damn! This is going to be tricky.'

'You can say that again.' Wa-ku looked up in frustration.

Hathor went quiet as she contemplated the situation. 'What do we do, Maru?' she pleaded.

The bland white glow of the Moon filled the window with its myriad craters pockmarking its surface. The shaded part rolled into view as the ship made swift progress towards the quadrant where their comrades were hidden. Numerous other ships also converged on the sector, and already they could see eruptions of light emerging from afar as the battle began.

Hathor turned to face Wa-ku and her expression softened. 'Soon, they will be so busy battling that we can slip away when the moment is right. Well, that's our hope.'

A flash of light whizzed past them as a duoculi ship fired on them. Hathor spun the ship into a tight turn that put them on the outer edge of the battle. A fleet of duoculi ships fled away towards the asteroid belt closely pursued by the tresoculi ships. Some failed to make it as plasma bursts found their marks, creating silent explosions as ships disintegrated into a thousand metal shards. A few tresoculi ships also succumbed as adept gunners took them down.

'I know what they are doing,' Wa-ku said. 'Our ships are using the asteroids to make it harder for the tresoculi to get them.'

Hathor accelerated them towards the asteroids and their own ships. 'We have an idea,' Hathor said, concentrating on the visuals, and playing the crystals like some strange instrument of music.

'Hide us behind the asteroids?' Wa-ku asked.

'You'll see,' she said.

They flew in between misshapen rocks that were spread around like so much litter. Flashes of light burst up from varying places amid the asteroids as combatants played a lethal game of hide and seek.

Hathor swung her head towards Wa-ku and indicated a crystal array on the other side of the command room. 'Love, press that red one in the middle over there when I tell you.'

He positioned himself in front of the array and poised his hand over the indicated crystal.

The ship swung into alignment with an asteroid. 'Shoot!' she commanded.

Wa-ku pressed the crystal and immediately felt a jolt as a plasma beam shot out towards the asteroid. It struck a jagged section of rock which splintered off like a projectile towards whatever was hidden on the other side.

'Watch it *Isis Five*! You nearly got us. What are you doing?'

'Our apologies. Thought we saw one of the duoculi ships duck behind there,' Hathor said, intoning a man's voice.

'Yeah! We were about to engage it. We had it in our sights until you spoilt it,' an angry voice returned.

Wa-ku chuckled. 'Clever move.'

Hathor smiled briefly before turning her attention ahead again. She pressed against a dark crystal and a holographic image of asteroids sprung into view in the air to the right of her. She swivelled the image and used her index finger to draw lines between the objects, resulting in angles and calculations that showed up along the lines that she drew. Wa-ku watched on with amazement as Hathor fiddled with the calculations and drew more lines before closing the image by wrapping her hand around it.

'Prepare for another shot, darling,' she said.

They accelerated towards a collection of smaller asteroids that clung loosely together. Intermittent flashes erupted all around as though an invisible storm was at play in space. Hathor flung the ship around in a tight curve, always keeping the group of asteroids in front of the ship.

The ship drifted across the space in an arc, propelled by its momentum until Hathor judged the angle was right.

'Shoot!' she shouted.

Wa-ku pressed the crystal, and immediately a plasma beam shot out towards the collection of asteroids and struck a small one on the outer edge. The elongated asteroid spun into the others, creating a domino effect as each smashed into another and propelled an asteroid on the other side to be flung out like a spinning bullet into space. Several tresoculi craft were in pursuit as they passed into the space corresponding with the trajectory of the errant asteroid. Since their attention was focused wholly on the pursuit of duoculi craft, they did not notice the asteroid that was on a collision course with them. The large rock hit the first ship with such force that it spun out of control into another ship then both ships hit a third ship. The three exploded as the asteroid caught up with them, littering its surface with debris.

'That takes care of one of the command ships,' Hathor said. 'Now, we need to get back to Nerthule before anyone notices us missing.'

Wa-ku shook his head. 'I don't believe that just happened,' he said. 'How did you do that?'

Hathor smiled. 'It helps when you have an Ancient working with you.'

Hathor turned the ship around and accelerated towards the tiny blue dot bathed in space. But, as they passed the orbit of Mars, several duoculi craft locked onto them and went in pursuit.

'I need to call them off us. What are the ships?' Wa-ku said.

'No need. We can outrun them, love. If we call them off, the tresoculi will get suspicious.'

'You got a point there,' he said, eyeing the screen nervously as the ships closed in on their path.

Hathor increased their speed, shooting them ahead at such a rate their vision blurred for a few seconds, and the blue dot quickly took form into a planet with swirls of white and blotches of brown. If it wasn't for the G-force stabilisers, their bodies would be crushed against the walls. It was one thing that Nerthulians had yet to learn.

PYRAMID OF POWER

Ra noticed the glint in the Einuk stone. 'Who has taken my stones here!' he said aloud. The meridians in the pyramid pulsed with the voices of the perpetrators.

'Hail Mirrortac! You have the stone?' said one.

'Nay! Einuk is in the hands of the one called Ra. He has a great shining pyramid ...' another went on.

Ra fumed. 'How did that creature come here so soon? And who is the duoculi who dares bring these other stones?'

The name of an unfamiliar Ancient calling herself Hathor echoed inside the chamber. Ra listened intently as Kelly confirmed his suspicions about him being an Ancient.

'Such vulgar language ... kick my ass indeed. That will not be so easy, Mister Kelly!'

The meridians abruptly stopped pulsing and the glint in the stone dissipated.

Ra sent his thoughts racing to his fleet of cosmo-ships. *All commanders in orbit. A duoculi ship carrying our precious stones has entered the system. It is paramount that you intercept and destroy it, then collect the stones and leave them on Mars.*

A chorus of voices answered to the call. *Your command be done, oh holy Ra!*

Ra knew that Kelly and the furry ones were nearby as Einuk had linked with the crystal that the roznogh carried on her. He also knew that if Oashu and Darm were within a few hundred metres of Einuk, the combined energy would be of such enormity that anything in the vicinity would tremble with the power. Only an Ancient would be able to withstand such power without falling ill and dying. As long as Einuk was inside the pyramid, the other two stones posed no danger, as even in the extremely unlikely event that the Ancient could enter with the stones, their explosive power would be neutralised by the pyramid's own metal and crystalline energy field.

The communication soon came that some of Ra's cosmo-ships had been destroyed or severely damaged and the *Petrichor* had disappeared into the asteroid belt. Ra hoped that it had crashed, as the ship was reported damaged in the attack. His Nerthule surveillance fleet had kept an eye out for the *Petrichor* but there was no sign of the ship after several hours. The only encounter was with a duoculi ship called *The Thor* which was engaged by *Isis Five* on patrol in the area between the Moon and Nerthule. Details of the encounter were sketchy at best as the captain had not submitted a report. However, Ra deduced that since *The Thor* was in the vicinity, that the duoculi had more ships hidden nearby. The tresoculi command ship *Horus* revealed that *The Thor* had appeared from the lee side of the Moon and that there were likely an entire fleet hidden there. Ra issued the command to engage the duoculi ship, which was directed to all ships in Nerthule orbit while the fleet above Egypt remained to destroy any of the Nerthulians' flimsy craft.

Now that the *Petrichor* was out of action, Ra could focus on his visitors on the ground. He would make them think they had the advantage by inviting Kelly to enter the pyramid unimpeded. Without the Ancient's assistance, the furry ones would be at a loss to do anything. Kelly had disguised his position among the Ancients admirably and had carried off his crude Australian identity with aplomb. Ra was impressed but knew that Kelly could assist his purpose.

The elder erfin gazed up at the pyramid with something close to awe. It was so high that a wisp of cloud clung to its cool peak. On the side where the sun shone on its surface, the metal cells glared with such brightness that one had to look away or wear what the Nerthulians called 'shades'. But Mirrortac's head was too wide to accommodate them, and his ears were in the wrong place for the handles. There was a ripple reflection in the force field that surrounded the edifice as Kelly frowned and regarded his colleagues.

'Ra wants me to go in. He is opening the field for me to enter,' he said.

Mitac's eyes narrowed. 'It's a trap. Don't go.'

'I know it's a trap, but I can turn it on him. I am Einuk's keeper ... maybe I can wrench the bugger off him.'

'We will come with you,' Mirrortac said.

'He won't allow it. You need to wait out here. We need the other two stones, and Hathor. You can't be anywhere near here when the stones are brought in.'

'What?' they all chorused.

'Believe me, little mates. You will die if you stay on the ground.'

'Die? How can that be?' Mirrortac said, scratching his head.

'You have played your part, and for that we are grateful. But you cannot handle the stones when they are so near each other. The energy is just too much.'

'But what about you? Won't it kill you?' Mitac said.

'No. I'm an Ancient. We created these stones in the first place.'

Mirrortac shook his head with disbelief. 'You took us all this way for naught!'

'Not for naught, my friends. We need to get you out of here and safely back home. I can only do that if I have you with me.'

'Then we will come with you to Ra.'

'You can't, simple as that!' Kelly said with an edge of impatience in his voice.

Mirrortac recalled the disturbance caused when Ameece and he and the hyfnuks removed Oashu on its own. The building it was in shook as though hit by an earthquake. Perhaps Kelly was right.

'Be careful, James Kelly,' Ameece cautioned as Kelly turned away and walked towards the shimmering force field.

They saw him disappear for a moment before reappearing on the other side of the field. He strode across the sand the last 100 metres before a stone slid open on the side of the pyramid, allowing him entry.

##

Kelly's eyes adjusted to the darkness within the pyramid. The air was surprisingly cool and fresh, but as he climbed the stairway to Ra's chamber, his head began to feel heavy as he breathed in a strange scent that numbed his mind. Each step became laboured as he tried to focus. The alarm bells were clanging in his drugged mind that he had to turn around. But it was too late. He fainted as the edges of the numbing scent overtook him.

Kelly could not tell how long he had been unconscious, but his head still felt heavy.

'Ah, T'in-ka, you come as a lamb to the slaughter. My power is already much more than any Ancient can stifle.'

Kelly felt the drowsiness wearing off as he forced open his eyes. He found himself laying on a bed hollowed out of stone and surrounded by clusters of yellow crystals. He tried to lift himself up but discovered he didn't have the strength.

'Shit, what have I got myself into,' he lamented.

'Indeed, your knowledge has waned within your earthly form, T'in-ka. That is your name, isn't it? I see you have learned nothing since we first met in the ancient days of Atlantis. You presume to overpower me within the temple where my power is greatest. Foolish man. I have foiled your plans. The ship carrying the stones is lost, and with it this other Ancient whose real identity is yet to be revealed. And now you will assist me in your duty and look into the Pool of Knowledge so there may not be any more surprises,' Ra smirked at him.

'And what makes you think I'm going to look into the Pool of Knowledge? Maybe it'll be the Pool of B-S instead.'

Ra leaned down until Kelly could feel and smell his breath. 'You will do as I say, or I will destroy your friends and all of the army that waits at my door.'

'Okay, but I need the power of Einuk to focus my mind and spirit.'

'Do you take me for a fool, T'in-ka. The energy of this temple will suffice, and if that will not do, then the vision of your friends dying will.'

Kelly arched up an eyebrow at Ra. 'It won't do you any good, you know. The Pool of Knowledge is always in flux ... it is only a raw indication at best.'

'Then it should be no concern for you to do as I ask.'

Kelly grunted as he tried to move. 'Okay, I will do it. Just let me off this thing.'

Ra pushed on one of the crystals and all of them sunk back into the stone out of sight. Kelly felt his strength return. He pushed up on his arms and swung his feet over to the floor.

'I still need a focus crystal. I don't suppose you have one?'

Ra waved his arm towards a pedestal in the chamber where a large sapphire coloured crystal radiated a soft luminescence. Kelly shook off the last of the numbness as he made his way to the pedestal and placed his hands on each side. He then held the crystal without lifting it and shut his eyes. He took several deep slow breaths before seeming to drift off into a sleep state.

In his mind, he repeated the sacred mantra that only the Ancients knew. It was just moments before he felt his body release him and send him drifting out of view of the chamber and into a dimension of light and the sound of sighing ethereal noise. The outlines of human figures coalesced around an enormous bowl that was filled with sparkling stars and fluid shapes of things that had been and are yet to come. The form of an elder woman emerged out of the many Ancients who dwelt here and approached him. She took his hand and looked steadily into his eyes.

'T'in-ka, do not be perturbed. You will look upon the Pool of Knowledge, but first I will tell you what I have seen there. This is how we will overcome Ra.'

Maru whispered into his ear as she led him to the Pool of Knowledge, and what he heard clearly disturbed him as he gasped at the telling, and when he was finally standing at the edge of the great bowl, he hesitated to stare down as the pool revealed its truths to him. Finally, he turned to Maru with a sad face and said, 'Is there no other way? There must be another way!' he said, looking at her with imploring eyes.

'It is what must be. You have done all that is possible. Now you must leave it to destiny.'

Kelly returned to himself and opened his eyes. He wiped at a tear as he turned to Ra.

'I have seen the signs of destiny within the Pool of Knowledge, and it causes me to tremble to reveal its secrets to a power-hungry dipstick such as yourself,' Kelly said between gritted teeth.

Ra smiled. 'Your humanity is amusing, T'in-ka. Now, tell me what you saw. What challenges do I face with destiny?'

Kelly sneered as he looked up at Ra with moisture tinged eyes. 'The war between our peoples will end with the loss of many many lives on both sides; and this world will be severely affected. Your challenge will boil down to a battle with the erfin Mirrortac who will achieve the impossible in defeating you. The only way you can prevent his success is to give up Einuk to my hands now. If you do not, then you may see victory in your grasp, but it will be an illusion.'

Ra laughed. 'You underestimate me, ancient one. Do you think that I can believe this tale of yours and will hand over Einuk to you? You are an even greater fool than I thought to think I will swallow such lies.'

A small smile appeared on the Australian's face. 'If you will not accept what is true, then you are doomed already, Ra. I swear to all the holy writ that what I say is the truth as revealed in the Pool of Knowledge.'

Ra gave him a dismissive wave. 'How can one of these furry creatures ever win over the might of one such as I? No. I will not believe such a thing. But since you believe it, I will ensure I destroy him first, then there can be no mistake. And these others of his kin I will take and use their mind powers to bring all the world under my rule. This world is mine, and soon the triad will arrive to give me absolute rule.'

Kelly sighed and bowed his head. 'Yes, the triad of Mareos, Thenigmas and Nerthule will soon arrive but ...' He could not continue.

Ra saw the defeat written on the Ancient's face and detected victory. 'Aha! There will be no challenge. I am the god of Atlantis and now of all the world! There will be no "but".'

'As you say, Ra–Ra. Now, since I have peeked into the Pool of Knowledge for you, I will return to my colleagues.'

Kelly stood and started to walk to the chamber door when Ra shouted back at him. 'You will go nowhere, T'in-ka. You are my "insurance" as this world calls it. I cannot allow you to cause mischief out in the desert.'

Just then the pedestal holding the crystal began to shake followed by a thunderous sound that reverberated through the floor. Kelly felt his feet shudder and he found it difficult to stand. Ra frowned as the walls vibrated and the shaking became so intense that the crystal snapped off the pedestal and fell onto the floor, shattering. Ra turned with a look of alarm and ran out of the chamber and onto the stairway up to the main chamber where Einuk was housed.

Kelly swayed as he tried to run after him, slipping and falling as he clambered up the steps. He got to the top panting and puffing as the tremor continued. Ra was inside staring at Einuk which was glowing a brilliant red. Kelly stumbled in just as the tremor lessened and the glow in the stone was subdued.

Ra turned and glared at Kelly. 'You did not tell me everything, did you, T'in-ka? So be it! I will destroy all of you!'

* * *

Kelly had been gone for some time when Mirrortac noticed one of the tresoculi ships descending from out of the sky. It was directly above them as the five of them sought to shelter inside the APC.

'We have no need to be sucked up into the enemy vessel,' Mirrortac said, climbing into the back of the APC.

Treetam was the last to enter when she halted and stared with open mouth towards the pyramid. 'O-M-G!' she said. 'There's a cloud on top of the pyramid ... it looks like a storm!'

Four furry heads poked out of the doorway of the APC to see what Treetam was talking about. It was as she had described – grey-green scuds of cloud were forming over the apex of the pyramid and rapidly thickening. They had all forgotten about the alien ship that still descended over the area, and even the soldiers camped nearby had their attention focused on the pyramid. Treetam trembled and instinctively leaped off the ground as though something had bitten her, but before Ameece could ask her what was wrong, they all felt the APC starting to vibrate. A loud grinding came from beneath the sand accompanied by a violent tremor that shook everything around them. The sand of the desert appeared to dance above the surface, creating a dust cloud that rose and obscured the army camp with its vehicles, marquees and personnel. Lightning was flashing from the cloud to the apex of the pyramid mountain, accompanied by loud claps of thunder that tore through the air.

I am sorry. The greater good must prevail, Hathor voiced in their heads. Her tone was filled with regret.

They had no time to consider these words when the dust and the storm disappeared behind a shield of light that shone directly upon them. Within a breath all the world was gone, and they found themselves standing inside the alien craft in company with Wa-ku and Hathor.

'Welcome aboard my furry friends,' Wa-ku said with a grim expression.

Hathor was stroking and pushing on crystals that sent the cosmo-ship back up into the stratosphere where it hovered in geo-synchronous orbit over Africa. On the floor were the combined Stones of Destiny of Darm and Oashu which were glowing pink. Hathor stopped her operations and turned to them. Her long strands of dark hair were tied up in a bun on top of her head, and her eyes spoke of compassion and sorrow.

Before she could speak, Wa-ku quickly intervened. 'Oh, you have not met Hathor, nurse and now one of our Ancients.'

Mirrortac and the others nodded lightly.

'We have just saved your lives, but at the loss of hundreds of the Nerthulians who were camped alongside the Pyramid of Ra,' Hathor said.

Ameece and the erfins exchanged startled looks.

'What do you mean?' Mitac frowned.

She sighed. 'We had to get close enough to pick you up, and in so doing, the powerful energy of these stones here and Einuk interacted to create an explosion that killed every living thing within a large radius around the pyramid. We could not warn them as that would have alerted the other tresoculi to our presence, and they would have destroyed us and, as a result of the stones dropping to the earth, everything in the vicinity.'

Mirrortac threw up his hands to his face. 'You saved us few to kill the many!' His voice quivered with anger.

Hathor drew up to him and put her hands on his shoulders. Then she spoke softly. 'We saved the few to save many many more. Without you we cannot hope to complete this mission.'

The erfin lifted his face and looked up at her with tears in his eyes.

'Mister Kelly said we have done our part. It is now up to you to bring the stones together. You are the only Ancient who can abide the power of these stones.'

Hathor was silent for a few moments before choosing what to say. 'This ship is a tresoculi ship. I am the only one who can operate it. I cannot leave here.'

'Then who ...?' Mirrortac's words stuck on his tongue, and the others all looked aghast at the Uranian woman.

Hathor was at the verge of tears herself as she sucked in a sob. 'Yes ... only you, Mirrortac, can take the stone to Einuk.'

Ameece shook and stepped up to Hathor. 'No! No! He will die! He cannot do this!'

The triplets started to clamour and shout at Hathor and Wa-ku; Ameece was in hysterics.

Hathor turned away and burst into deep sobs. 'I don't want to do this anymore!' she cried. But in an instant, her sobbing subsided, and she drew herself up to her full height. Her demeanour had changed, and it was clear that this was no longer the pretty, fragile nurse speaking.

A deeper woman's tone measured out words like pearls. 'Do not hold this woman to blame. I am the ancient one who they call Maru, and it is in this erfin's destiny to play this part in the mission set for him since he came upon the frosted lands of his ancestors. It seems that something of our ancient power has been bestowed upon him and will provide sufficient protection for him to complete his mission. It is true that the force exerted on him will be so great that his life in your plane will be greatly shortened, but by how much I am not at liberty to reveal. We had no idea until consulting the Pool of Knowledge of this erfin's role, nor would we have believed it had it not been revealed to us with such definition that it cannot be doubted.

Without him, Ra cannot be defeated ... and without you, your father, partner cannot survive.'

The presence of the Ancient Maru left Hathor, and she again fell into a ball on the floor and wept. There was a stunned silence as all sat and considered what was said to them. Treetam was the first to stand up and wrap her arms around the woman who moaned with her head sunk between her knees. Wa-ku also comforted her, and Hathor threw her head into his lap.

Mirrortac and Ameece nuzzled each other in silent contemplation, and as he lifted his green eyes to look into hers, there was a sense of acceptance and resolve that brought peace to his features.

'This is what I must do, rainbow of my heart. We cannot allow this Ra to overwhelm these peoples. All our destinies are linked.'

Ameece sucked in a long breath and smiled at her loved one. 'I know,' she said.

Mirrortac stood and went to pick up the two Stones of Destiny. 'I am prepared. Take us down so I can complete this task.'

It was Wa-ku who spoke this time as Hathor still sniffled in his lap.

'We cannot go just yet ...'

'What now?' Mirrortac stamped his foot but regretted it as soon as he felt the pain shoot up his leg.

'The danger has not passed ...'

Mirrortac shook his head but Mitac interjected.

'A great war has begun,' Mitac said, hardly believing what he was saying. 'Listen Dada, everyone. Listen to the Nerthulian rulers.'

Through the clamour of minds, they picked out the rulers of the leading nations, and they were all speaking of nuclear arms. The obliteration the stones caused in Egypt had spread panic among the nations. China, the USA and Russia were launching nuclear warheads aimed at the Pyramid of Ra. All the world's nations had agreed to a total war against the alien menace and were not discriminating between duoculi and tresoculi; to them all were to be eliminated without regard. The Ancients knew that these weapons were sufficient to create enormous destruction and death, and not the clean quick death offered through plasma blasts. This was a toxic cloud that was so lethal that even those who survived the blast would slowly die from horrendous necrotising wounds that went into the blood and spread their lingering death to all the cells of the body. And as if this was not enough, the many millions of Nerthulians who now followed the way of Ra were instigating guerrilla attacks on the major cities of the world.

Mirrortac slumped down in despair. 'Must I wait for these death-bringers to take the lives of more Nerthulians? The triad of the worlds must be nearing. It will soon be too late.'

Wa-ku cleared his throat and looked away. 'It is already here ... the triad is here,' he croaked.

Mirrortac slammed a fist into a wall. 'What! Then we can do nothing!'

'We still can eliminate Ra as well as destroy the Stones,' Wa-ku said.

'We'll get rid of Ra like we did Yidu,' Ezof enthused.

Hathor raised her head from Wa-ku's lap. 'Your bravery is noble, little one, but Ra will not be defeated so easily.'

'How will you bring the stones together without them exploding in your face?' Mitac said.

Hathor sighed. 'That will be difficult. But if Mirrortac can use these stones as a portal connection, then he can transport himself inside the pyramid and call the stones inside. They will not explode as long as they are inside the pyramid, but they will connect and become one stone.'

'Then I can use the portal from here,' he offered.

'No. You must be on the ground and close enough to the pyramid ...' Hathor could not finish.

'... to cause much thunder and kill more Nerthulians,' Mirrortac replied.

'No, there are no more Nerthulians near the pyramid,' she said, 'but you need a portal stone such as Ra possesses to call in the two stones. That means you must port into the pyramid first then overcome Ra to gain his portal stone.'

Mirrortac scratched his furry head. 'What? Do I use the two stones as a gateway, then use another stone that Ra has to bring the two stones into the pyramid?'

Hathor nodded. 'Yes, he should have the stone on a string around his neck or in a pocket on his robe. It will be the same colour as the Werdstone on Mareos.'

There was a long pause before Mirrortac spoke again. 'And what of the triad? Is it not too late now?'

Mitac stroked his beard. 'The triad is the link of the three planets, no?' he asked.

Hathor and Wa-ku nodded.

'What makes this link?'

'The three planets er ... the Stones of Destiny,' Hathor said.

'Would not the stones need to be on Mareos and Thenigmas to link the three?' he mused.

Hathor and Wa-ku paused as their eyes widened.

'Ah, I see ... two stones are here ... with us,' Hathor brightened.

'No triad!' Hathor and Wa-ku said in unison.

'But Nerthule will be under Ra's complete power as long as all the stones are here,' Hathor said.

'The link to the Werdstone will concentrate all the power in Nerthule,' Wa-ku added.

Through the screens set in place in the cosmo-ship they could see out to space and witness the arrival of the second fleet of duoculi ships. The void soon filled with the flashes of war in the heavens, and the flaring trails of craft fatally hit. It was like a fire show that from a distance was almost beautiful in its sparkles of coloured light and bright flashes. But each feathery radiance of red and blue and yellow displayed the deaths of a crew of Uranians. Below them, in the north of the continent of Africa, the first nuclear warheads made their impact. Brilliant clouds rose high into the atmosphere like giant thunderheads that foamed upwards and outwards. Could Ra survive this? The Uranians knew the answer was yes. Despite the destructive power of these weapons, the force field generated from Einuk and the pyramid repelled the explosive waves that flattened all in its path, and sent it rippling back like the side of a pond – back across Egypt and to its settlements and towns. Ra's fleet of cosmo-ships ranged over the globe, blasting at armies and cities with abandon. However, they were not immune to the warheads. Some managed to hit their mark or explode in the air near them, destroying their ships.

It was soon evident to the Nerthulians that the nuclear weapons were more damaging to them than Ra. Instead, military campaigns were launched against the "New Atlanteans" and Ra's army of Thenigmas warriors and erfins. These were easier to kill, but they were now counted in their millions.

* * *

Six days passed after war began, and it was now considered safe enough for Mirrortac to enter the zone around the pyramid. They were about to prepare for his entry when the communication monitor came to life.

'*Isis Five*, prepare for boarding!'

Hathor adopted a male voice. 'Sir, the transfer plate is damaged. You cannot board.'

'*Isis Five*, this is the *Horus*. We know there is nothing wrong with the transfer plate. We are coming on board.'

'With respect sir, what is your business here?' Hathor waved frantically at the others to hide in the aft ship storage chamber.

Wa-ku gathered up Ameece and the erfins and took them down a hallway.

'You are supposed to be engaged in battle, yet you have returned here to Nerthule orbit. We suspect that you are duoculi who have pirated our ship.'

'Sir, our ship sustained damage and that is why we had to return to orbit for urgent repairs.'

'We are coming aboard now!'

'No, you're not!' she yelled in her own voice.

Hathor accelerated out of orbit and shot into space away from the pursuit of the *Horus*, but her move was too late. Four men armed with solar-bites appeared on the transfer plate.

'Maru, where was your warning about this?' she muttered under her breath.

My dear sister, Destiny hid this from you, came the reply.

Hathor glared back at the tresoculi officers.

A sneer appeared on one of the officers. His face was misshapen, and he was missing an arm. His third eye shone red like lava from a volcano.

'Such a pretty one. Perhaps we should take out our pleasures on her before we kill her.'

Hathor paled, and her blood ran cold. 'Beast! I will kill myself before I would give my body to any of you.'

The men laughed while the one-armed man stepped towards her. Hathor backed up against the crystal wall, trying to retreat from the man who approached.

This only spurred him to block off her getaway with his bulky hairy left arm. She could smell him now. His body odour wafted over her as he pressed himself against her.

'I have not introduced myself. I am Adius, head officer in charge of the *Horus*. I know you want to play, my sweet,' he said, licking his lips and sliding his body over her tight-fitting pants.

Hathor tried to push him off her, but he only pressed harder against her. The other men were ogling her too. Adius began to loosen his robe when he abruptly stopped and stepped back.

Come and get us. We will give you what you want, he-man.

Hathor heard the voices in her head. They sounded like women's voices.

'Who is that?' Adius said. The other men flicked their heads around to see who was speaking in their minds.

Come on big boy, we are a crew of women. Don't bother with Hathor. We are so much tastier. Find us!

Adius looked with a satisfied leer at the other men. 'Did you hear that? They want to play with us, brothers. Let's get them!'

The men left the control room and started searching the hallways of the ship.

Hathor breathed out and wiped away tears. She could hear the men tramping down the hallways and opening hatchways and calling out. Then there was a thud and the sound of a struggle.

Wa-ku glided out of the hallway and embraced her. 'Are you all right?' he said, fussing over her body to ensure she had not been abused. She nodded while more scuffling sounds echoed up the hallways.

'We've managed to knock them out, and the erfins are tying them up,' he said.

'What the hell are you creatures?' a man's voice shouted.

'Well, almost all of them,' Wa-ku corrected.

There was another thud followed by silence.

'Mmm, I think that's all of them now,' Wa-ku said.

Hathor's eyes slid across to a monitor above her head, and her eyes widened. She abruptly jumped up and stared at the screen.

'What is it? Not more visitors?' Wa-ku said.

Hathor turned her pale face towards him. 'No. Worse. We are being targeted.'

Wa-ku glided across to the screen. 'Can we outrun it?'

Hathor engaged the pulse drive and shot them out of range beyond the planet. The missile thundered up into the stratosphere following their trail, but its slow rise was no match against the propulsion of a tresoculi ship. It faulted as it entered space and its yellow tail extinguished before the missile exploded. There was a brilliant flash then darkness again.

'We are not safe. We are not safe,' Hathor muttered.

The five appeared puffing from out of a hallway.

'We sure took care of them,' Ezof grinned.

'They should be out to it for a while,' Treetam added.

Mirrortac strode up to Wa-ku and looked at him expectedly. 'Now, can I take the stones down now?'

Wa-ku shook his head. 'We have another problem. The Nerthulians are shooting at us. We cannot come close enough.'

'Perhaps one of those smaller capsules will not be shot,' Mitac ventured.

'Smaller capsule?' Wa-ku and Hathor chorused.

THE TERRIBLE STORM

Ra's golden helm glinted in the light of the meridians that populated the inner walls of the Einuk chamber. His breathing slowed as the many lines changed hue and more joined them in a green glow surrounding him. Occasionally, there were points of yellow and red and blue sparking up from the wall, like a silent symphony that brought joy to the demi-god's eyes. His lips parted, and a breath went out to the world. Millions of Nerthulian devices came to life as the face and voice of an alien master-being made ready to communicate a message to them. Kelly stood by in helpless awe, his head hung low, as the meridians ushered in the transformation.

'Silence your minds, my wayward servants,' Ra began. 'Do not fret any further. Do not poison yourselves with your weapons. Awaken to this new age as I have come not to enslave you but to grant you abilities beyond your imaginings. You all know of me from your ancient Egyptian archaeology. God of the sun ... and why is that? Because I can harness the energy and transmit it to you all without the need of ungainly wires and polluting mechanisms. I tried to free you once before at Atlantis, but you were not ready. Give up your superstitions of lesser gods for I am the one you seek. This Pyramid of Ra will provide all the energy you need. Shut up your radio and television stations and instead tune in to the one and only truth. Forget about your primitive talking devices. I will teach you all to speak with your minds. But I do warn you that any who seek to deny me will instantly die. Any who seek to cast weapons upon me and my sacred ones will die. Come to me now, receive your gift of precious crystal that will show that you are my followers; and to those who already are my followers, rejoice.'

The transmission appeared to have an immediate effect as the meridians pulsed with gratitude and incantations of praise and worship. The bombing halted, and many converted on the spot. Only some of the poor and most primitive, or those who shunned technology, eluded the conversion. They had no knowledge of what had happened. However, a cosmo-ship called the *Isis Five* was identified as an enemy, and all efforts were to be made to destroy it lest it endanger the souls of the converted. Ra knew that the ship would elude the missiles but as long as it stayed in space, its threat was nullified.

Ra instructed his armies of warriors and followers to demolish all primitive fuel sources and make all inhabitants dependent on his energy generating pyramid. More energy pyramids would be built to supply the whole of Nerthule, and all communications systems would be placed under his control. Democracy would end as all governments would be disbanded and only the United Nations would stand to inform him and spread his commands to the world.

Kelly sat in a corner of the Einuk sanctuary meditating constantly. Ra merely laughed at him and continued with his plans for Nerthule. Occasionally Kelly cocked an eye at Ra before returning to his meditation. He was calm.

* * *

It was on a night several weeks into his full reign that Ra felt the first tremor. It was only slight, like the passing of a heavy vehicle on a road, and it soon was gone. But in the early hours leading to dawn, there was a second tremor. This time it did not pass but kept up a low rumbling vibration that unnerved him. Kelly did not stir from his sleep. Ra got up from his own bed and rushed to where Einuk was glowing a soft pink.

'How can this be?' he muttered.

He pressed his fingers into a crystal array that activated his communication meridians.

'Awaken my children! It seems the enemy has entered our presence while we were asleep. He travels alone and is intent on desecrating the most sacred temple with his vile objects. Seek him out across Egypt and execute him! You will recognise him from his white fur and alien creature appearance.'

'We serve to rid the earth of this defiler. All hail Ra!' the voices answered.

##

The pods settled on the rough sandy ground near the Pyramid of Menkaure where its gaping gash mocked the erfins as they alighted from their space vehicles. The late afternoon sun shone gold on the faces of the nearby pyramids. Mirrortac glared back at the triplets as he trudged bearing the weight of Oashu-Darm in his two arms.

'Go back to your mother. I must do this alone!' he said.

'You need us,' Mitac called out. 'What if someone attacks you?'

'You will die from the poison cloud.'

'I know where we can gain protective wearables. Kelly told me ... it is inside this man-stone mountain – the pyramid. Find the camel creatures to travel the desert.'

Mirrortac frowned but his eyes betrayed his pride for his children.

The elder erfin began to search the nearby area while the triplets approached the pyramid. Earthen robed Egyptian men roamed nearby, and armed guards lifted their rifles towards the erfins in a hostile attitude.

'We are on an errand for the most holy Ra,' Mitac explained, prompting the guards to lower their rifles and perform a blessing on their foreheads.

The three left the tiled path and ascended a stairway that led into a small opening into the pyramid. Artificial lighting provided a clear view inside where they found their way down into an area that had been sealed with a transparent flexible material, with a separated access antechamber stocked with hazard suits. They picked up four of the suits and returned outside to rendezvous with Mirrortac who by this time had managed to find two camels that he had purloined from their keeper who was napping under a makeshift shelter. The suits were tight on their chests and waists but crumpled down due to their short stature.

Mirrortac stashed Oashu-Darm into a saddlebag on one of the camels and struggled onto its back as it lay with its knees bent on the sand. Treetam got on behind him while Mitac and Ezof mounted the other camel. Wa-ku had supplied each of them with solar-bites, and food and moisture tablets for the journey.

The camels rose with groans of complaint as the lights of the city of Cairo switched on in the gathering evening. The camels' keeper awoke and chased after them, muttering curses, but to no avail. Chants to Ra rose up in place of the traditional Muslim utterances as the small caravan made its way through the outer urban areas before reaching the desert proper. Curious onlookers regarded the suited interlopers as they passed by, most realising that they were headed to the contaminated zone some distance to the west. Soldiers patrolled the city streets but ignored the erfins in their suits.

Mitac thought out to the others. *Ra does not know we are here.*

The service pods did the job, Treetam replied.

Yeah, and Hathor guided us down to the peer-mid, Ezof added.

Mirrortac cringed as the camel loped over the sandy ground. *When the earth shakes, Ra will know. You must stop when the shaking throws you off your beast. I alone will continue.*

Treetam hugged the elder erfin through his suit. *We will go as far as we can, dada.*

He turned and patted his daughter, his eyes invisible behind the window of his hood.

They travelled throughout the night as the glow of the stars reeled over their heads, bright and mesmerising away from the lights of Cairo. The night grew cold but the erfins' fur and hazard suits provided ample protection. Lizards and small rodent type creatures scuttled about in the darkness, but mostly went about their activities without being noticed. Dawn came like a warning as they regarded the dust cloud that obscured the view of the western horizon. Scavenger birds wheeled over distant carcasses – of animal or human they knew not, but their great numbers were a sign of much death ahead. Mirrortac brought his camel to a halt and dismounted. The brothers did the same as they paused to rest the animals and eat.

The suits were starting to feel hot and uncomfortable as the temperature of the day rose. Mirrortac took off his hood as they were still a distance away from the poisonous cloud, but the sharpness of the mid-morning heat and the absence of a breeze gave little respite.

Soon they were on their way again, but the elder erfin had not yet replaced his hood. He was again watching the birds as they plunged down to the earth and squabbled among themselves for the prime pieces of meat. As they neared the carcasses, they could see that they were mostly that of camels and birds and small mammals. Mirrortac donned his hood and heard his breath accentuated as he clipped it down tight. The roiling cloud was now within a few camel strides.

Ezof surveyed the cloud with fear as it enveloped them and took them into a place of darkness where they could only see a few steps in front of their camels. The sun was reduced to a pale orange ball above them. Dust and a grey ash settled on their suits and camels, which began to grunt and slow their pace. They had to urge their mounts onward to gain any distance as the camels were inclined to bed down against the onslaught of dust and ash. They struggled on throughout the day with no relief from the cloud.

The camels began to stumble against bodies of people, goats and more camels, then there were the remnants of dwellings and vehicles. The litter of bodies and materials accumulated across the sands before they negotiated up and down dunes. There were no birds or animal cries here – only desolation.

On the second night, the sky was clear again. They had passed the poison cloud, but the landscape was scoured with the clutter of death. They rested again until the Moon rose, then resumed their trek west. When their camels began loudly complaining, almost refusing to go ahead, they all realised that the tremors had begun. It was slight at first, disguised by the loping gait of the camels, and it all but disappeared for a while before returning shortly before dawn. The continuous vibration under their feet unnerved the camels and sent them into a panic. The creatures turned and loped towards the east for some distance before the erfins could bring them to a stop.

Mirrortac dismounted. *We can go no further on these beasts. Take our supplies from them and tie them down so you can go back on them.*

He assisted Treetam from the back of the camel while Mitac and Ezof dismounted and grabbed their food supplies. Oashu-Darm emerged from the saddlebag glowing pink and felt warm as Mirrortac used both his hands to take the weight of the combined stones. However, before the erfins could secure the camels in any way, the beasts panicked again and ran off into the desert.

There is no way to tie them down, anyway, Mitac said, shrugging at his father and indicating the bare ground.

Hmmm. I am supposing they will die when I come close to Einuk. If only we had taken that stone when we first came into that house of ancient objects, Mirrortac said.

Nobody answered.

They turned to the west and started to trudge through the thick sand as night made the journey more comfortable again. They could feel the constant grumble under their feet and slipped as the tremors unsettled the dunes, sending streams of sand avalanching down their sides. The tremors gathered strength with each step they took, and they often had to claw their way out of sand drifts that almost buried them.

Dawn came with the clouds – dark churning bubbles that foamed out of the west along with the constant grinding of the earth. The erfins knew this was no natural phenomenon; as with each step nearer to Einuk, the forces between the Three Stones of Destiny were building up their power. The stones were not meant to be this close to each other, and now the combined energy of Oashu and Darm were acting against that of Einuk.

Mirrortac shook and fell as lightning shot out from Oashu-Darm and struck the clouds, creating loud booms that shook the air so much that it smacked against their ears like rocks.

He stared up at his three children and shouted, 'You must turn back now! I must go on alone!'

The three looked back with sad eyes, knowing that their father was right.

I heard the people talking about us, Mitac said. *They saw the 'white erfin' with us ... you, dada. They know where you are and are searching to find you.*

We will stop them, dada! We will tear off their heads and smash them into the ground! Ezof enthused.

Take care, dada, Treetam said, lifting her hand to offer the signal that the Nerthulians use to say goodbye or hello.

Mirrortac stood again and took up Oashu-Darm in his arms. The triplets swivelled around and began retracing their steps towards those who came to stop the elder erfin's mission. When he arched his head around again to take a last look at his child-fins, they were nearly out of sight disappearing behind a dune.

'It is just you and I again, oh dark one,' Mirrortac said, as he started up the next dune.

* * *

As silent as the grim reaper, the drone coasted over the cream hued landscape, its camera eyes examining anything that moved on the sands below. This drone was one of many scanning the desert country. Safe in their operations centre in Cairo sat trained technical officers of the Egyptian armed forces. Each man was poised in front of a screen that displayed what each drone saw as it flew its course. Anything of interest was recorded and displayed on a separate screen for scrutiny. Specific frames could be magnified many times until even the smallest insect could be identified, and its coordinates mapped out.

After several hours of observation, one of the officers called out. 'Sir, there are three ... um ... people in hazard suits walking together.'

The head officer examined the screen. 'Is there a fourth person ... carrying a heavy object? I cannot see him.'

'No sir. It seems there are only these three, and they are only carrying supply packs. And they are all walking the wrong way.'

'Mark their position and move on. We have no time to waste. We must find the stone carrier.'

The officer nodded and pressed some buttons to record the position before guiding the drone to continue its flight further west.

The head officer stood alongside the monitor. 'He cannot be far away. Our most venerable Ra is only a day's walk from this position.'

'Converge all drones to run a close parallel path from this position to the holy pyramid, and arm missiles ready for firing,' he commanded.

A chorus of 'Yes sir!' rang out from the room.

It was just a few minutes before the same officer called out again. 'Sir, I believe I have located the carrier. He is within 20 miles of the holy pyramid.'

The head officer, who was striding back and forth across the row of monitors, returned to examine the screen of the officer who had called out. 'Good work. You may fire when ready.'

The officer began to place a fix on the erfin, but the camera sight blurred and shuddered violently, making it difficult to lock on to target. Another officer called out 'A drone has exploded'.

'What do you mean "a drone has exploded", officer Abdul?' the head officer screamed.

'Sir, I sighted the three co-conspirators then one flashed something, and the drone blanked out ... exploded.'

'Blast! Never mind. We have found the culprit. Now why isn't he dead yet?'

'Sir, the drone is experiencing severe turbulence from the storm. I am trying to get a fix on him.'

'That must be some storm!' The head officer turned towards the others. 'Converge on the unholy one's coordinates, boys, and press those fire buttons. If it misses, it will still kill the bastard!'

'Right! Sir!' they shouted together.

All drones were targeted to the one position and their missiles sent to auto-detect body heat.

'Fire now!' the head officer commanded.

Red firing buttons were exposed and pressed. Nine missiles shot out. The drone within sight of the erfin saw him take cover before the screen was blotted out by a blinding flash, and all vision of the scene lost.

The officer announced his last finding. 'Target dead. Mission completed.'

Rousing cheers filled the room. The head officer performed a blessing on his forehead. 'Oh, venerable and most almighty Ra. It is done.'

##

Ra smirked as the news of Mirrortac's demise reached him. He glanced over at Kelly who was huddled in a corner of the room with his head bowed. The tremors in the pyramid were making it impossible to stand.

'I must go out and dispose of those other stones,' he shouted. 'Your precious erfin is dead. And soon you will be too.'

Ra negotiated the long stairway down to the entrance to the pyramid, clinging to the railing as the edifice shook one way then another. He struggled out into the darkness outside as a lightning storm struck at the faces of the pyramid. He covered his mouth and nose with his cloak as sand whirled in eddies over the ground.

He took out a small crystal and fingered it, immediately sending him flying across the earth towards the combined destiny stones. In moments, the curved form of the two stones materialised in the sands ahead of him. Under the stones was the prostrate figure of a white-suited erfin clutching the stones in front of his face.

Ra wrenched the stones from the body and began to walk away with them towards the east. The lightning storm did not abate as he climbed one dune after another until he encountered three hazard suits half buried in the sand. They were torn with large tufts of grey fur spread around them. Nearby were three bodies burned beyond recognition.

T'in-ka, your colleagues are all dead. The meddling erfins are now just ashen cinders in the desert, Ra transmitted to Kelly.

Only an empty silence filled with deep sadness answered the demi-god. He felt nothing for the Ancient nor his friends and continued his way through the desert.

* * *

Kelly edged his way out of the pyramid as black clouds foamed and bubbled above him.

Lightning tore down and struck him in the chest, throwing him in a tumble onto the sand. He stumbled to his feet and trudged a few metres before being struck down again. Any normal human being would be flat out unconscious but not this Ancient. He endured the direct strikes with grunts as each hit winded him temporarily before he could stand again and push on. The skin on his hands was singed as he held tightly on to the glowing Einuk stone. He was determined to finish what Mirrortac had begun. He was determined to avenge the deaths of four brave erfins, even if it meant his own death.

Sand blasted at him and stung any exposed skin. He could hardly see where he was going after being blinded so many times by the lightning. He brushed up against something soft and looked down at the still form of an erfin.

Don't worry, little mate. I'll finish this for you, he thought as he plunged on ahead.

Each step now was agony as he forced himself up a tall dune. His robe fluttered violently, and each lightning strike hit with more power than the last, bowling him down to be almost buried in an avalanche of sand. He dug his way out again and again, but his battle barely gained him a few metres each time. His arms and legs were aching from the effort, and his face above the mask of cloth was smudged with dirt wet from his own tears. He tried to cry out, but his voice was lost in the wind and thunder and rumbling earth. He collapsed from the effort and watched as the grey columns of sand whirled around him. Everything was a confusion of dark shapes and noise; he even fancied seeing something moving past him up the dune, but it soon disappeared in the flurry of other shapes.

Kelly tried to breathe but the sandstorm was suffocating. He shut his eyes from the stinging grains and tried to regain his strength. *Come on, you bludger! Get the hell up and save the day!*

* * *

Ra couldn't understand why the fury seemed to be worsening even though he was taking Oashu-Darm farther away from the pyramid and Einuk. It was so bad now that lightning was striking at the combined stone and knocking him off his feet. He remembered that he had left Kelly alone with Einuk, and the annoying Ancient was likely following him with it. He started to run to put more distance between them, knowing that it would be easier for him to move away than it would be for Kelly to move closer.

The demi-god slid down the other side of a dune in a flash of gold as his robe fluttered in the wind. As he crossed each dune, the storm started to wane a little although the ground still shook constantly. He could feel Kelly's energy flagging and it was possible that he had stopped moving.

Once he was far enough away, Ra decided to rest for a few minutes before alerting one of his cosmo-ships to come and collect the combined stone and take it out into space. He rubbed the sand out of his eyes and shook the dust from his cloak then looked out to the east across the rolling dunes.

Come secure the stones. It is Ra who commands it.

We are sending the 'Jackal', oh revered one, came the answer.

Ra was about to stand when a large furry arm wrapped around his neck and started to choke him.

'Be not moving, oh wretched one!' came a familiar voice.

Ra struggled against the erfin but Mirrortac was strong. *You are dead! How can this be?*

'These stones protected me from the boom tubes.'

You are too late, erfin. In a few moments, my men will take me up in their ship and these stones and you will be dumped on the other side of this solar system.

Mirrortac tightened his grip. 'Then you shall come with me, oh wretched one!'

The erfin heard the whirring of the cosmo-ship as it descended towards them, and its beam shone down to envelope them both. Mirrortac grasped at a crystal around Ra's neck and clutched it in the palm of his hand. He muttered something incomprehensible before they both disappeared.

##

'What are we going to do with these tresoculi?' Hathor said, referring to their four prisoners.

Wa-ku looked out at the star-screen. 'Throw them into space,' he offered.

It had been some time since the erfins had left in the escape capsules.

'Do you not have them punished where you come from?' Ameece asked.

'Yes, yes, of course,' Wa-ku said. 'But we will need to transfer them to one of our other ships where they can be better guarded.'

Hathor smiled. 'That was clever of you to pretend to be women to lure them away from me. You saved me from those beasts!'

'Oh, that was Treetam. Mitac thought of the idea and Treetam did the mind-talk thing,' Ameece said.

'Well, I'm glad you thought of it, otherwise we would be their prisoners, and they would have ...' Hathor shuddered, unable to finish what she was saying.

Ameece approached and wrapped her arms around her waist. 'Do not think on it. You are safe now.'

Hathor hugged her and kissed the top of her head.

Wa-ku glided across in his chair to join them. 'What amazing creatures you are,' he said.

'Oh dear!' Hathor was suddenly distressed.

'What is it?' Ameece and Wa-ku chorused.

'The Nerthulians are attacking the erfins. They are after Mirrortac!'

'What with? They cannot enter the desert with the tremors and storms from the stones,' Wa-ku said.

Ameece frowned. 'Flying thunder?'

Hathor nodded. 'Drones ... they have cameras – eyes – that can seek out an enemy and then blow them up with missiles.'

'We must save them! I cannot have my child-fins dead, and my love.'

'Can we move closer now and beam them in, perhaps?' Wa-ku ventured.

'Yes! We could try. But not Mirrortac, I'm afraid. He still has the stones,' Hathor said.

Hathor hastened as she worked the crystal controls, bringing the ship down at startling speed before opening the beam to take in the triplets. The desert dunes were soon in view on the monitor before they sighted the triplets as one of them used a solar-bite to destroy a drone.

She pressed on one of the crystals. 'Okay, beaming them in.'

The triplets disappeared from the ground and reappeared moments later on the transfer plate. The three threw off their protection suits as Ezof exclaimed, 'Woo! I was not ready for that!'

All of them gathered around the monitor as Hathor manoeuvred around to the west to sight Mirrortac struggling with the stones as the drones converged on his position. Missiles shot out from the drones as the erfin crouched down and hid his face under Oashu-Darm. There was an enormous flash as all the missiles exploded in mid-air, knocking the erfin into the sand.

Ameece threw her hands up to her face and let out a wailing cry. 'My dearness!'

Treetam and Ameece fell into each other's arms and wailed loudly while the others looked on in shock.

After a long pause, Wa-ku said, 'Ra will come for the stones. He will want to send them far away.'

Hathor brushed away a tear. 'That's right. We need to stop him, but how?'

'Would he know about us being nearby?' Mitac asked.

'Ra would have sent the drones. They saw you. Ra saw you.'

'But did he see us vanish from the sandy hills?'

Hathor shook her head slowly. 'No.'

'Then we were killed,' Mitac said.

Wa-ku raised a brow. 'Then we need three bodies ... burnt beyond recognition.'

'For verification,' Hathor chimed in.

Ameece rubbed her hands together in agitation. 'You mean to kill those three-eyed ones we have back there?' She indicated the hallway behind her.

Hathor bent down and looked Ameece in the eye. 'They would have us all killed in the blink of an eye. If Ra comes into the desert, he must not suspect that we came to rescue your children. He would have us shot down if he knew.'

The roznogh's eyes were downcast. 'We must do what we must do,' she said, almost whispering.

All their eyes strayed back to the monitor as they sighted Ra appear beside Mirrortac and wrench Oashu-Darm from his grasp. Hathor sensed Kelly's sadness as Ra walked away with the stone, and but a few minutes later, saw Kelly emerge from the pyramid carrying something. He paused beside the prostrate erfin before continuing in pursuit of Ra.

'He's trying to complete the mission – to bring all the stones together,' Hathor said.

They watched as the turmoil grew around the Ancient and struck him down repeatedly, slowing his progress.

And then, a miracle. The body of the erfin moved and clambered to his feet.

They all gasped with awe and relief as Mirrortac started to walk east, passing Kelly who was so caught up in the storm that he had not noticed the erfin walk past him. Finally, the Ancient gave up and started to walk back to the pyramid with the object he carried.

'He must have Einuk with him!' Hathor said.

'Quick, get three of the tresoculi and put them on the transfer plate.'

The triplets and Ameece went down the hall and collected three of the tresoculi men and placed them on the plate as requested. Wa-ku hovered over towards them and drew out his solar-bite. The men were still tied up and gagged. Their accusing eyes stared back at Wa-ku in defiance.

'You might not want to see this,' he said.

The others turned their backs as Wa-ku fired at the three men and incinerated them.

'Put your hazard suits on the plate and pull out some of your fur and put it there too,' Hathor commanded.

They gathered the hazard suits and threw them on the plate then pulled out bunches of their fur. Ameece choked back vomit as she looked around at the blackened bodies and smelled the burnt flesh. The triplets cast bits of their fur over the remains before retreating in disgust.

Hathor activated the transfer plate, and in moments the blackened mass had faded into a mist before disappearing. In the monitor, the remains coalesced on the sand dune where the erfins had been minutes before. Ra was still advancing across the dunes to the west while Kelly retreated to the pyramid.

Hathor glanced around at the others. It was clear to all that the Ancient Maru was in control. 'I must tell T'in-ka that Mirrortac is alive, that we are all alive. There is also something that Mirrortac needs to know before he reaches Ra.'

Hathor shut her eyes as she focused on contacting Kelly and Mirrortac.

T'in-ka. We know you have Einuk. Do not despair; the erfins are all alive. The Ancients know of a plan to finish this.

Kelly's voice entered their heads. *How can this be true? I saw the erfin dead on the sand. Ra was told that the others also died.*

Oashu-Darm shielded the erfin. He is now in pursuit of Ra. We took up the triplets before the explosions, Hathor said.

Kelly's mind was full of doubts. *But Ra will call on his three-eyes to take the stones away.*

Do not concern yourself, T'in-ka. Ra has made a fatal mistake. We will get him. You must go back inside the pyramid and place Einuk back where you found it. Then prepare for a surprise visit.

Hathor redirected her mind to Mirrortac, who was a white patch moving up and down the dunes.

Mirrortac! It is Hathor. We have further news to assist you when you reach Ra. When you grab the link-crystal around his neck, the words you need to port to the pyramid will meld in your mind. Do you understand?

The erfin allowed a smile as he took in this information. *I know what to do, great one,* he said.

AN EXPLOSIVE COMBINATION

Kelly hastened up the stairway with renewed hope in his heart. Einuk was still glowing as he crossed the uppermost chamber and placed the stone back on its pedestal. It seemed that all around him coloured stars twinkled from the chamber walls, each one a person captive to the will of Ra. There were billions. The tremors that had started days ago, now abruptly stopped, replaced by an awful brooding silence. The stars too were extinguished so that it was darker than a moonless night.

Kelly watched Einuk turn a deep violet before he could hear something like a rushing wind moaning through the chamber. A ghostly light appeared in the shape of a tall man and an erfin clutched together. There was a violent shudder then a thump as Ra and Mirrortac appeared near the pedestal. The combined stones that Ra struggled to cling onto were flung out of his grip and immediately attached to the side of Einuk, completing an oval of three stones together. The force of the adhesion caused the two to sprawl together on the floor.

'I'll take that, thank you mate,' Kelly said as he grabbed the Stones of Destiny from the pedestal and started for the stairs.

Ra jumped up and tackled the Ancient, dropping him. 'No, not so fast, T'in-ka!' Ra growled.

They wrestled as Mirrortac gained his feet and advanced on Kelly. 'Give it to me. I will cast it to the wasteland,' he said.

Kelly tried to reach up with the stones, but Ra overpowered him and pinned him to the floor. Mirrortac jumped on Ra and smacked his head hard, sending the gold helm tinkering across the tiles. Then he started punching into him with his brawny fists. This allowed Kelly to extricate himself from under him. He struggled to his feet, and still holding on to the now combined stone, made another attempt at the stairs.

Ra used his third eye to produce a brilliant flash that temporarily blinded the erfin. He stood but instead of running after Kelly, turned and walked back to the pedestal where he laid his hands and began to mutter an incantation. There was a loud grinding accompanied by a sinking sensation as the pyramid moved downwards into the sands of the desert.

Kelly tumbled down the stairs with a series of thumps and grunts. He saw the exit grow darker as the pyramid sunk below ground level. Still stunned, Mirrortac lumbered towards the pedestal and Ra. He felt himself going numb as the demi-god stared intently at him. He wasn't going to make it. Clinging vainly to consciousness, his legs gave way beneath him and he slumped to the floor.

With his last moments of clarity, Mirrortac decided to try something he had not done since his departure from Hopocus where he had defeated the dark sorceress Helok and her partner, Krak.

He would leave his body.

His meditation soon took him into the greater dreaming that he remembered. This time, there was no spiritual helper to greet him. His consciousness hovered within the chamber like a mist. He could see Ra who was looking down on his erfin body with a grim smile. He thought of Kelly down below and was immediately there. The Ancient was struggling to open the exit door, but the weight of the sand outside was thwarting his efforts. *I must rise the pyramid,* he thought.

In a flash, he was back at the pedestal where Ra stood contemplating his next move.

Ra was using the maja tongue when he made this pyramid sink. I wonder if I can do it without my bodily vessel.

Mirrortac saw a field of energy around the pedestal that responded to the demi-god's own energies. The field had a life of its own, flowing in streams of ochre and yellow through the air and out of Ra's fingers. Then he saw his own energy – in fact he was all energy – flowing and whirling in an endless stream. He touched the pedestal and saw that the energy field was disturbed and redirected. He directed his thoughts to move the energy, and it responded. He tried first to move it away from the pedestal, toying with it as though brushing colours through the air. Ra shuddered and started to look around him.

'Who is there? What is this?!' he accused, flinging himself around like a man blindfolded.

The erfin began to swirl the energy around in increasing circles, causing it to brighten like a flame. He balled it and directed it then flung it at Ra with such force that he let go of the pedestal and stumbled backwards.

T'in-ka! Are you doing this?

Doing what, you arrogant toad? came the reply.

You are playing with me. It will do you no good. You cannot escape!

Wanna bet? Kelly teased.

Mirrortac saw his mirth bubble out in green bursts of energy as he listened in to Ra and Kelly's exchange.

He contemplated the flow of energy and saw that one stream was flowing from the demi-god's hands across the floor and down the stairs. Even though he could only see it, the energy's purpose was clear – push down on the pyramid. It was a mass of red earth energy that appeared as thick as magma and glowed with enormous strength.

Mirrortac concentrated on reversing the flow, and gradually, the brilliant stream slowed before stopping. The erfin pushed and massaged at it to move upwards. When at last, the stream changed its direction, he heard Ra becoming agitated. Ra started muttering in maja and pushing the stream back. Mirrortac converged the energy towards the pedestal and swung it at Ra as though he were hurling a heavy metal ball at him. The demi-god was flung to the floor. Ra cursed and activated his third eye, which scanned the room like the beam from a lighthouse. The beam paused as it detected the erfin's presence.

It cannot be! It cannot be! How can you be there erfin when I left you drugged on the floor?

I have learned much on my journeys, dark one, Mirrortac replied.

Ra got up from the floor and regarded him with his third eye. *Indeed, you have. Even the Ancients do not have such power. I could have much use for you, my friend. You could join me in governing this rabble of humanity. They have weak minds and will destroy this Earth without our guidance. You and I will make great rulers.*

Mirrortac's soul chuckled, sending out bubbles of green energy. *I have no need for such things, dark one. I only wish to return to my old home of Eol when this is all finished. I see you as you are, surrounded in darkness.*

Darkness is free, darkness is safe, whispered Ra.

Darkness blinds, darkness imprisons, Mirrortac said.

The erfin gathered all the energy again and whirled it upwards in a tornado that rotated faster and faster and faster until he flung it in one massive vortex at the ceiling. A loud clap like thunder rocked the pyramid and flung it up above the ground in a violent surge. Ra was hurled up at the wall like a rag doll, and Mirrortac saw his own body thump against the ceiling before coming to rest once more on the floor.

That is going to hurt, he thought, inwardly wincing.

Kelly rubbed his head after hitting the ceiling above the doorway. He wasted no time gathering up the Stones of Destiny and opening the door to the outside. Positioning himself near the threshold, he gained all the strength of his arms and tossed the stones out onto the sand. He had hardly begun to shut the door again when he had to shield himself from a flash so bright that it seemed to permeate every cell of his body. The explosion that followed deafened him and shook the pyramid with sufficient violence to puncture the side that faced the conflagration. Fragments of metal rained down outside; super-heated air drifted in through the doorway opening in a shimmering wave, and Kelly felt his shoes melting under his feet.

The Ancient jumped up as the heat burned his feet. A glaze formed over the floor and walls, crystalising silica into glass where all the sand had blasted in. Kelly ran up the stairs to escape being burned and entered the uppermost chamber just as Mirrortac regained consciousness. Ra was sitting up on the floor holding one of his legs that was bent at an unnatural angle. He muttered a healing incantation between moans and cries of pain.

Kelly looked at the erfin dumbfounded. 'What just happened here?'

Mirrortac gave a mysterious smile and said, 'I put the energies backwards.'

The Ancient looked askance, his eyes going from side to side. 'You're a dark horse, that's for sure, little mate.'

Mirrortac chuckled. 'Rather, I be a light horse, James Kelly.'

The two laughed as Kelly regarded Ra with a sneer.

'How the mighty fall,' he said.

'Spare me your Nerthulian tongue, T'in-ka.'

They bound Ra's arms behind his back and took him down the stairs to the exit. As they stepped outside, they were confronted with a deep hole of glassed silica that glinted in pointed shards. Heat still shimmered up from the hole into a clear blue sky. The *Isis Five* was directly above them, while nearby was the wreckage of the *Jackal* that Ra had previously called to dispose of Oashu-Darm.

Moments later they were aboard ship with Hathor, Wa-ku and the others. Ra was dragged into a secure holding room with the remaining officer from the *Horus*. Mirrortac had tinges of grey in his eyebrows and through the fur on his face. Ameece embraced and nuzzled him while the triplets waited their turn to greet their father. Hathor and Wa-ku looked at each other and at the elder erfin with a smile on their lips.

'You have done it, Mirrortac. I would not have believed it had I not witnessed it,' Wa-ku said.

'And you too, James Kelly,' he added, turning towards the Ancient.

'No worries, my friends,' Kelly said with a wink.

He extended a hand towards Hathor. 'We shake hands as a greeting where I come from here.'

Hathor took his hand then drew him up to her in an embrace. 'I believe hugs are a better greeting where you come from.'

'Too right, as long as your boyfriend here doesn't get jealous,' Kelly said.

Wa-ku swung around and hovered over to Kelly. 'I would give you a hug too, James Kelly, but a handshake will have to do.'

Kelly leaned down and wrapped his arms around the Uranian in his chair. 'Nah, you won't get out of it that easily, mate.'

Hathor resumed control of the ship. 'I best get us out of here before the Nerthulians start shooting at us again. After all they have been through, they will not feel too friendly towards any of us.'

Kelly nodded. 'Yeah, guess you're right. It's time for me to return home, anyway. But I'm going to miss the place.' He looked back at the monitor as the ground retreated from view, and the brown form of the continent of Africa took shape through the clouds.

He waved at the monitor as his hand brushed at his eye. 'You're on your own now, buddies. Take care.'

Treetam stared up at him and nuzzled his chest. 'You're a big softie, James Kelly.'

'That I am.'

An escort of duoculi craft surrounded the *Isis Five* as they left the Earth's atmosphere and entered space. All the tresoculi craft remaining had already left the solar system for Kosmo. Kelly sighed as Hathor glided the ship past the Moon, and they exchanged a knowing glance.

'We will take you back home, my little mates, but for us the war has just begun.'

'The three-eyes?' Mitac asked.

'Yep. They have lost Nerthule and will be fighting to conquer the ruling duoculi at our home planet Kosmo.'

Treetam enveloped Kelly's arm. 'Stay with us. You are not warriors.'

'Maybe Wa-ku and Hathor can stay with you. But I am an Ancient. They need me.'

'I too am an Ancient,' Hathor said. 'They will need me also. And they will need nurses.'

'It is our home. I hate the idea of war, but Hathor is right – they'll need her, and where she goes, I go.'

Hathor strode over to the communication terminal. 'Meanwhile, in case you have all forgotten, we must transfer back to our own ship, the *Petrichor*.'

'Oh yes,' Wa-ku rubbed his hands together and his eyes lit up. 'I can be useful again, instead of wandering around like a lost pup.'

'And I can give up flying this crystal monstrosity,' Hathor added.

* * *

A sea of curious eyes stared up as the *Petrichor* descended onto a courtyard alongside a marbelite temple. On one side were wide steps going down towards a village of primitive huts, while the archways and pillars of the temple provided a backdrop to the alien craft that had landed in its midst. Shadowing the village rose three peaks covered in snow and draped with a skirt of fir trees. Fields of nif-grass nodded in a soft breeze, laden with grain. Barely visible to the south was the glistening waters of a lake.

A group of tentative grey erfins ventured towards the marblelite steps, and among them were two females whose eyes furtively searched the ramp that descended from the craft. A silvan white elder emerged with a walking stick, and beside him a white furred female held his arm. Three more grey erfins followed them along with two tall beings and one in a floating chair.

A scream rose from the crowd as two erfin females broke rank and ran up the steps to embrace their parents and siblings.

'Papa!' Fentil cried. 'We knew you were naught dead!'

The other daughter, Wynper, joined the embrace with a burst of tears. 'And who be this?' she said, pointing at Ameece.

The white roznogh's face was moist with her emotion at seeing them. 'I am your mother reborn. I so remember making flatbread before the fire for you. Then that he-erfin of mine had to find a damned sword in the woods!'

Wynper and Fentil screamed and embraced Ameece, then their siblings Mitac, Ezof and Treetam.

That night there was feasting for those who had returned, and a special welcome for the visiting Uranians. Mirrortac gave Wa-ku a cheeky grin as he presented him with tufts of grey and white fur.

'Give this to the one named Fayth so she can put this on her head,' he said.

Wa-ku regarded the erfin with a little confusion as he gingerly accepted the fur. 'For her head?'

'She likes our fur ... for something called "fashion",' he explained.

Wa-ku broke into a wide grin. 'Ah, she will love it, I'm sure.'

The next morning, as a light mist shrouded the community of Eol, the three guardians bid farewell and ascended into the Greater Sky.